TREASON

BOOKS BY STUART WOODS

FICTION

Treason*

Stealth*

Contraband*

Wild Card*

A Delicate Touch*

Desperate Measures*

Turbulence*

Shoot First*

Unbound*

Quick & Dirty*

Indecent Exposure*†

Fast & Loose*

Below the Belt*

Sex, Lies & Serious Money*

Dishonorable Intentions*

Family Jewels*

Scandalous Behavior*

Foreign Affairs*

Naked Greed*

Hot Pursuit*

Insatiable Appetites*

Paris Match*

Cut and Thrust*

Carnal Curiosity*

Standup Guy*

Doing Hard Time*

Unintended Consequences*

Collateral Damage*

Severe Clear*

Unnatural Acts*

D.C. Dead*

Son of Stone*

Bel-Air Dead*

Strategic Moves*

Santa Fe Edge†

Lucid Intervals*

Kisser*

Hothouse Orchid‡

Loitering with Intent*

Mounting Fears§

Hot Mahogany*

Santa Fe Dead†

Beverly Hills Dead

Shoot Him If He Runs*

Fresh Disasters*

Short Straw†

Dark Harbor*

Iron Orchid‡

Two-Dollar Bill*

The Prince of Beverly Hills

*Reckless Abandon**

Capital Crimes§

*Dirty Work**

Blood Orchid‡

*The Short Forever**

Orchid Blues‡

*Cold Paradise**

*L.A. Dead**

The Run§

*Worst Fears Realized**

Orchid Beach‡

*Swimming to Catalina**

*Dead in the Water**

*Dirt**

Choke

Imperfect Strangers

Heat

Dead Eyes

L.A. Times

Santa Fe Rules†

*New York Dead**

Palindrome

Grass Roots§

White Cargo

Deep Lie§

Under the Lake

Run Before the Wind§

Chiefs§

COAUTHORED BOOKS

*Skin Game*** (with Parnell Hall)

*The Money Shot*** (with Parnell Hall)

Barely Legal†† (with Parnell Hall)

*Smooth Operator*** (with Parnell Hall)

TRAVEL

A Romantic's Guide to the Country Inns of Britain and Ireland (1979)

MEMOIR

Blue Water, Green Skipper

*A Stone Barrington Novel

†*An Ed Eagle Novel*

‡*A Holly Barker Novel*

§*A Will Lee Novel*

***A Teddy Fay Novel*

††*A Herbie Fisher Novel*

TREASON

STUART WOODS

G. P. PUTNAM'S SONS
New York

PUTNAM
— EST. 1838 —

G. P. Putnam's Sons
Publishers Since 1838
An imprint of Penguin Random House LLC
penguinrandomhouse.com

Library of Congress Cataloging-in-Publication Data

Names: Woods, Stuart, author.
Title: Treason / Stuart Woods.
Description: New York : G. P. Putnam's Sons, 2020. |
Series: A Stone Barrington novel |
Identifiers: LCCN 2019046075 (print) | LCCN 2019046076 (ebook) |
ISBN 9780593083192 (hardcover) | ISBN 9780593083215 (ebook)
Subjects: LCSH: Barrington, Stone (Fictitious character)—Fiction. |
Private investigators—Fiction. | GSAFD: Suspense fiction. |
Adventure fiction.
Classification: LCC PS3573.O642 T74 2020 (print) |
LCC PS3573.O642 (ebook) | DDC 813/.54—dc23
LC record available at https://lccn.loc.gov/2019046075
LC ebook record available at https://lccn.loc.gov/2019046076
p.   cm.

Printed in the United States of America
1   3   5   7   9   10   8   6   4   2

BOOK DESIGN BY KATY RIEGEL

TREASON

Stone Barrington was sitting up in bed watching last night's recording of *The Rachel Maddow Show*, while skipping Joe Scarborough's rant during the first half hour of *Morning Joe*, which was on a subject he had heard about too often: small government. His cell phone rang, and he picked it up. "Hello?"

"Scramble," a female voice said.

He paused. This was the secure cell phone on which he only got calls from Lance Cabot, the director of the Central Intelligence Agency, who always scrambled. It was a CIA iPhone, given to Stone when he was appointed special adviser to the director, with the putative rank of deputy director, though he was no such thing.

"Scramble, goddammit!" she said.

Stone pressed the button. "Scrambled," he said. "Now who the hell is this?"

"It's Holly, you complete ass," she said. "You don't recognize my voice anymore?" They had been lovers for years.

"Of course I do, but how did you get this number?"

"You gave it to me," she said, "to use for the most confidential calls, and all of my calls to you are most confidential."

"Oh," he said. Holly was the secretary of state and about to announce a run for the Democratic nomination for president. She was very, very careful about being seen or heard communicating with Stone; the press would have far too much fun reporting ad nauseam that she was sleeping with someone.

"'Oh'? Is that all you've got to say?"

"Yes," he replied. "Now it's your turn: What have you got to say?"

"I'm coming to New York, and I want to spend the night at your house, doing what we always do there."

"Oh."

"Oh, what?"

"Oh, of course. I look forward to seeing you. What time?"

"We're landing at the East Side Heliport at noon. Can Fred meet me?" Fred Flicker was Stone's factotum, a pint-sized veteran of Britain's Royal Marines Commandos.

"Sure. What did you mean by 'we'?"

"The presidents will be aboard, too, since it's the presidential helicopter." The presidents were Katharine Lee, the current president, and her husband, Will Lee, the former president.

"Invite them to dinner."

"I don't want to dine with them, I want to dine with you. Alone. I need your advice on something."

"Something that can't be discussed on a scrambled CIA iPhone?"

"Certainly not. Do you trust those people?" Holly had once been the director of the Central Intelligence Agency, and she knew them well.

"Well, yes, I trust them. Sort of."

"You're hopeless," she said. "See you later." She hung up.

Stone hung up, too, and the other phone rang again almost immediately. "Hello?"

"It's Dino. Dinner tonight? Viv is traveling again." Dino was Dino Bacchetti, Stone's former partner on the NYPD and now the police commissioner of New York City.

"Can't. Holly's on her way in for the evening."

"What, I'm not allowed to see Holly now?"

"She wants us to dine alone. She needs advice about something."

Dino made a snorting noise. "Advice? From *you?*"

"I give very good advice," Stone said. "My friends' lives would be so richer, fuller, and happier if they would just take it."

"You're delusional," Dino said. "Tomorrow night?"

"Sure."

"Patroon, at seven?"

"Sure."

Dino hung up.

Stone was at his desk at noon, waiting for Holly to arrive. Joan Robertson, his secretary, buzzed him.

"Yes?"

"Some woman claiming to be the secretary of state is on one. Shall I tell her to buzz off?"

"You know very well who that is," Stone said, pushing the button. "Where are you, Holly?"

"Out of the chopper and into the car. Since I spoke with you earlier I've been saddled with three pre-campaign chores that I have to take care of this afternoon. May I keep your car—and Fred?"

"You may. What time do you expect to finally land here?"

"By six, probably, which means maybe."

"I'll look for you when I see you coming."

"Great, bye." She hung up.

Stone called Helene, his housekeeper/cook and ordered dinner for seven o'clock, probably, perhaps later.

Helene understood. "It's moussaka; I can serve whenever."

"Good." Stone hung up and tried to find some work to do.

At seven-thirty, Holly called. "I'm on the way, there in ten." She hung up.

Stone called Helene and alerted her, then went up to his study to wait.

Sure enough, ten minutes later, Fred delivered her to the study, then took her luggage up to the master suite.

Stone and Holly wrapped themselves around each other and kissed noisily. She finally broke away. "Bourbon, now," she said breathlessly.

Stone poured them both one, and they settled onto the sofa before the fireplace, where a cheery blaze burned.

"Why don't we just down these drinks, strip off, and fuck each other's brains out right now?" Holly asked.

"Because Helene will be here shortly with our dinner, and we don't want to shock her and make her drop the dishes."

"Oh, well," Holly said, squeezing his genitals. "I'll just have to wait."

———

Dinner arrived, they sat down at the table, and Fred decanted the wine Stone had chosen. They tucked into their first course, Pâté Diana: goose liver with lots of butter.

"Okay, what advice do you need?" Stone asked.

"I have what you might call an administrative problem at State," she said.

"And we both are aware that I know absolutely nothing about the administration of the State Department, so why are you talking to me about it?"

"Because I trust your judgment."

"What judgment?"

"Judgment about everything."

"Even things I know nothing about?" Stone took a sip of his wine. "The reason some people trust my judgment is because I never give advice about things I know nothing about."

"Are you willing to listen?"

"Yes, of course. Shoot."

"I have reason to believe that there is a Russian mole in a trusted position at State."

Stone took a gulp of his wine and looked at her. She seemed absolutely serious.

olly took a gulp of her wine, too. "All right, now you know. What's your advice?"

"Shoot him between the eyes with a large-caliber weapon," Stone replied.

"Be serious."

"That's as serious as I can be with grossly insufficient information. Try again."

"My deputy secretary stopped by the house last night and insisted that we take a walk around the block, indicating with hand motions that there might be a bug in the house. So, we took a walk." She paused to stuff some moussaka into her mouth.

Stone waited for her to chew. "Did you check that out?"

"This morning. My living room was bugged. My people fixed it."

"And what did your deputy impart to you while you were hiking the streets of Georgetown?"

"That he believed there to be a mole in the department."

"On what evidence? And don't tell me a hunch."

"He had a briefing from somebody at the Agency whose report on the Russian situation contained a telephone intercept that em-

ployed the exact language he had used at a staff meeting at State a
week or so before."

"Who else attended the staff meeting?"

"About thirty staffers."

"How many State Department staffers are there?"

"A little over seventy-five thousand."

"So, you need only investigate the thirty? That's better than
seventy-five thousand. Why didn't you immediately call the FBI?"

"Are you nuts?"

"Isn't that what they do? Counterintelligence?"

"They would flood the department with agents, knocking over
things and looking into people's desk drawers and interrogating
my staff."

"Don't you think they know what they're doing?"

"I do think they know what they're doing, but they do it noisily,
and I can't afford that kind of noise right now. It would get into the
media before sunset tomorrow."

"Ah, so this has a political edge to it."

"Of course it has a political edge! Everything I do between now
and the election next year will have a political edge, whether I like
it or not!"

"I guess you're right about that."

"Then what am I going to do?"

"I don't know, what are you going to do?"

"That's what I need your advice about: What am I going to do?"

"Well, let's start by eliminating those actions that we feel
wouldn't work."

"Okay," she said, "start with the FBI."

"All right, number one. Don't call the FBI."

"Advice accepted. What else?"

"Well, let's see," he said, chewing his moussaka thoughtfully.

"Stop chewing your moussaka thoughtfully and come up with something!"

"Why don't you call somebody at the Agency?"

"Because Lance is out of the country, and I don't trust any of the other hierarchy there. If Hugh English got hold of this, I'd be hauled before the Senate Intelligence Committee the following day, put under oath, and made to look like a fool because there's a mole at State and I'm not doing anything about it!" Hugh English was the crusty old deputy director for intelligence, and he bitterly hated Lance—and Holly almost as much.

"All right, number two. Don't call anybody at the Agency."

"Advice accepted," she said. "What else?"

"Doesn't State have its own intelligence operation?"

"Yes, but since I don't know where the spy is in State, how can I trust them? He might be embedded in their ranks."

"Number three. Don't call in State's intelligence people."

"Jesus Christ. Advice accepted. Can't you come up with something that might have a chance of working?"

"It seems to me that you need a trusted partner in this, one who knows Washington well, knows where the bodies are buried, knows where to bury any fresh ones that turn up, and is a better counterspy than you or anyone else. In short, someone who would know exactly how to proceed."

"That sounds an awful lot like Lance Cabot," she said.

"As it happens, I have—right here in my pocket—a special telephone that will allow you to speak to Lance in a positively secure manner." He took out his Agency iPhone and put it on the dining table.

"I know," she said, digging into her purse and coming up with an iPhone. "I have one just like it." She put hers on the table.

"Then why haven't you called him already?"

"Two reasons," Holly said. "One, I wanted to talk to you before I made a move."

"Which you have now done."

"Two, I try never to make important decisions when my mind is really on sex."

"There must be something I can do to help," Stone said.

"Let's skip dessert," she replied, putting down her fork and heading toward the elevator. "Come on," she called over her shoulder.

"Coming, coming."

"Not yet, you aren't, but you will be soon!"

olly had, of course, been right. Stone lay on his back, taking deep breaths, while Holly fondled him further.

"If you're in search of an encore, you're going to have to wait a few minutes," he said.

"You must be getting old. I remember when it was always ready."

"You just dreamed that."

"All right," she said, withdrawing, "I'll be patient. Sort of."

"Maybe now would be a good time to call Lance," he suggested.

"Not yet. I haven't yet freed my mind of carnal thoughts."

"What are you going to do about that when or if you become president?" he asked.

"I'll call you," she replied smugly.

"What if I'm in L.A. or England or Paris?" he asked, naming the other places where he owned residences. "Or if you are?"

"I may have to resort to toys, but I'll need a lot of imagination for that."

"You want to pop down to the sex shop and pick out something just in case?"

"Not yet. You're available." She laughed. "See?"

She was right, he was stirring.

She held out her arms. "Come to me, baby."

He went to her. This time, she climaxed first.

Stone kissed her. "There, I've done my duty."

"That was above and beyond the call," she replied, kissing him back. "You have restored my faith."

"You were losing faith?"

"Let's just say it was wilting, but it's back now."

"Okay, time to call Lance."

"What time is it where he is?" she asked.

"I don't know where he is."

"Then how can we call him?"

"The phone works at night, too."

"But suppose it's the middle of the night?"

"Suppose Lance wanted to call you urgently: Would he hesitate if it were in the middle of the night?"

"All right, call him."

Stone retrieved his iPhone and pressed the button.

"Yes?"

"Scramble."

"Scrambled."

Stone pressed the speaker button and set the phone on Holly's naked belly.

"Lance, Holly's here with me."

"So I see," Lance replied.

"What?" Stone and Holly said simultaneously.

"Didn't I tell you that your Agency iPhone has a camera capability?"

"Every iPhone has a camera capability."

"All right, I was kidding."

Holly lifted the phone, and pulled the sheet over her breasts. Stone did something similar.

"Are we all ready to speak now?" Lance asked.

"Holly's deputy secretary—what's his name?"

"Mac," she said.

"Mac what?"

"Maclean McIntosh," Lance offered.

"That's the one," Holly said.

"What about him?"

"He took Holly for a walk in Georgetown and told her he thinks there's a mole at State."

"Turns out, my house was bugged," she added. "It's been fixed."

"What is his evidence?" Lance asked.

"One of your people sent him a document that included a phone intercept from GRU headquarters in Moscow. The intercept included language identical to what Mac had used when addressing a big staff meeting a week or so before."

"I know the intercept," Lance said. "I didn't know about the language."

"Only Mac would have recognized it, since it was his language," Holly said.

"Have you called the FBI?" he asked.

"Oh, really, Lance," Holly said, "it would be all over Fox News, or wherever, before the end of their first day on the investigation."

"You think the FBI leaks?"

"Sometimes," she said. "Their problem is, they don't blend in. They always look like FBI Special Agents."

"You have a point," Lance said. "Their presence would be disruptive, too."

"And I'd be yanked in front of the Intelligence Committee and asked why I haven't caught the mole," Holly added.

"There is that," Lance agreed.

"What should I do?" she asked.

"Stone, what do you think?" Lance asked.

"I told Holly I thought she should call you."

Lance sighed. "Everybody's last resort," he murmured.

"I called you the minute I . . ."

"The minute you what?"

"The minute I shared with Stone."

"I will let that one go," Lance said.

"I think what is needed," Stone interjected, "is an investigation that nobody knows is an investigation."

"What do you have in mind?" Holly asked.

"I don't have anything in mind," Stone replied. "I'm just positing something; it's not as though I have a solution."

"Then you're not positing anything," she said. "Look it up."

"Now, now, children," Lance said. "Holly, what Stone has, ah, posited is rather brilliant."

"It is?" Stone asked.

"I wish you wouldn't say things like that to him, Lance," Holly replied. "It will just puff him up."

"I have an operative who works in plain sight as a writer of nonfiction books. You may remember one called *The Tunnel Under the Pentagon*."

"About a mole in the Defense Department," Holly said. "But they didn't catch him."

"Suffice it to say the mole isn't there anymore," Lance replied. "I think it would be good if he spent some time at State, under the guise of researching another book—this one not about a mole."

"What do you mean by 'spend some time'?" Holly asked.

"I mean he'll turn up at Foggy Bottom, and you or Mac McIntosh will introduce him at a staff meeting and say that he'll be wandering around the shop and to talk to him. He'll have all the right clearances."

"What is his name?" Holly asked.

"He writes under the name of Martin Schell—likes to be called Marty."

"Oh, yes, I remember him," Holly said. "You remember, Stone."

"Never heard of him," Stone replied.

"Typical," she said.

"No need to tell you his real name," Lance said. "Suffice it to say he has a full legend, from birth through Yale."

"He went to Yale?" Holly asked.

"No, but that's what his legend says. If you call the registrar's office for information on him they'll have a complete file—his academic record, his degrees, the works."

"What if you asked someone who went to Yale when he was supposed to be there?" Stone asked.

"Do you remember all the names and faces of your freshman class at NYU?" Lance asked.

"I take your point."

"He also spent a couple of weeks soaking up the atmosphere in New Haven. He wouldn't be easily tripped up."

"Okay," Holly said, "he sounds great."

"But you can't tell anyone at State about him."

"What about Mac McIntosh?"

"Not even him. Marty will arrive with a folder of correspondence with you, and you can insert those into your files."

"When will he arrive?"

"He'll call your secretary and make an appointment."

"I'll be back in my office tomorrow afternoon."

"Fine. May I go back to sleep now?"

"Of course, Lance."

"And you two can go back to doing what you were doing," Lance said, then hung up.

Holly was looking carefully at Stone's iPhone. "Do you really think he could see us?"

After breakfast, Stone was still doing the *Times* crossword when Holly came out of her dressing room, dressed. "I'm off," she said, kissing him. "May I have Fred for the day? The chopper doesn't leave until four o'clock."

"Sure."

There was a knock on the door, and Fred appeared. "Is your luggage ready, Madam Secretary?"

"Yes, Fred, thank you. And you'll be driving me today, until four o'clock."

She kissed Stone again and followed Fred out of the room.

Stone arrived at Patroon for dinner, half a drink later than Dino, but a waiter quickly brought him even. He took a swig.

"How's Holly?" Dino asked.

"As ever," Stone said.

"What does she think about the mole?"

Stone gaped at him. "What mole?"

"The one Mac McIntosh says is loose at State."

"You're not supposed to know that," Stone said.

"Why not? I have the same clearances you do."

"You've been talking to Lance, haven't you?"

"You think Lance is some kind of blabbermouth?"

Stone laughed. "He is, when it's in his interests to be. When did you talk to him?"

"This morning, at breakfast."

"You had breakfast with Lance?"

"Isn't that okay?"

"I thought he was abroad somewhere."

"He was," Dino said. "Until he got here in time for breakfast. He was on an airplane from somewhere when you called him in the middle of the night."

"From where?"

"I've no idea. All I can tell you is he ate a big breakfast—eggs, bacon, pancakes—I don't know how the guy maintains his trim physique."

"Did he mention why he was telling you about Holly's mole?"

"He wanted my advice about what to do about it."

"Last night Holly wanted my advice, which was to call Lance. Now he's asking you for advice?"

"Yep."

"Then why don't you call Holly and ask her for her advice, then you'll have completed the circle. What advice did you give Lance?"

"I told him to find the guy, then take him out and shoot him."

"That was my first advice to Holly. The problem is finding the guy."

"Well, he's one of the thirty people who were at the staff meeting, right?"

"Maybe."

"Then give them all lie detector tests. That's easier than questioning all seventy-five thousand State employees."

"Don't you think the Russians—if it is the Russians—have trained him to defeat a polygraph?" Stone asked.

"Maybe. That would complicate things, wouldn't it?"

"I believe it would," Stone said. "Did Lance tell you what action he's taking?"

"You mean about the guy from Yale?"

"The guy who *says* he's from Yale. The Agency built that legend for him, and they're very good at that."

"How would you know?" Dino asked.

"I read spy novels, like everybody else."

"I don't read spy novels," Dino said.

"That's a lie. You've loaned me half a dozen over the years."

"I *used* to read spy novels," Dino said. "I found them entertaining, until I didn't anymore. I guess you're still reading them."

"I stopped reading them when you stopped loaning them to me," Stone said.

They both ordered the Caesar salad and the Dover sole. The salad was made tableside with considerable flair.

"What else?" Dino asked, when they were alone with their salads.

"Nothing else," Stone said.

"No new lady in your sights?"

"No new lady has crossed my path."

"And I guess the old flames are not speaking to you."

"That's a dirty, communist lie. I maintain good relations with my exes."

"Which must be hard to do, if they're not speaking to you."

"Change the subject, Dino."

"When was the last time an ex spoke to you?"

"Jesus, I don't know."

"Today? Yesterday? Last week?"

Stone sighed. "What else did Lance have to say for himself?"

"He told me about your elevation to— What is it? Private counselor?"

"Special adviser."

"Well, that sounds meaningless."

"With the rank of deputy director," Stone said.

"Hah! We know *that's* meaningless, don't we?"

"It was Lance's idea, not mine."

"He's just blowing smoke up your ass," Dino said.

"Why would he do that? You and I were both consultants, weren't we?"

"Yeah."

"Has he promoted you?"

"How can he promote me from a position that's meaningless?" Dino asked.

"Maybe it was meaningless in your case," Stone said, "but Lance and I talked quite a lot when I was still a consultant. Now we talk even more often."

The waiter arrived with their Dover soles, then another waiter set another place at the table, and a third Dover sole was put there.

"What?" Dino said. "Do we look that hungry?"

Lance Cabot slid into their booth and picked up his fork, while the waiter arrived with a second bottle of wine. "Good evening, gentlemen," Lance said.

"We were just talking about you," Dino said.

"Of course you were. What else do you have to talk about?"

"He has a point," Stone said.

"I'm sorry I didn't make it in time for the Caesar," Lance said.

"Quite all right," Stone replied.

"Have you two solved the problem of the mole at State, yet?"

"Not yet," Stone replied. "Dino isn't being very helpful."

"We both like your plan, though," Dino said. "The one with the Yale guy."

"I'm so pleased," Lance said. "Now, if you'll excuse me, I have to eat this sole before it gets away."

5

Holly was at her desk at State the following morning. Her deputy secretary, Maclean McIntosh, knocked and entered the room. "Good morning," he said cheerfully.

"Good morning, Mac," she replied. "Anything of note happen in my absence?"

"I had a note from the White House chief of staff that we're to host a writer, name of Martin Schell, for an indeterminate time. He's doing some research for a book."

"What sort of book?" she asked.

"Nonfiction, I gather. He must be pretty well connected."

"Mac, if I know you at all, you know exactly how connected he is and everything else about him."

Mac grinned sheepishly and opened a file. "Born in Boston forty years ago, attended Groton, then Yale, graduated summa cum laude. He's written half a dozen well-reviewed books featuring various government agencies, a couple of bestsellers. Divorced two years ago, no kids."

"That sounds pretty accurate to me," a voice said from the doorway.

Holly looked up to see a man—six-two, a hundred and sixty pounds, thick, longish salt-and-pepper hair—carrying a handsome, well-used briefcase and dressed in a tweed suit and a knitted necktie. "Let's see some ID, or I'll have to have you taken out and shot," Holly said.

He produced a letter from an inside pocket. "I'm Martin Schell. This is a copy of the letter you've already received from the White House chief of staff."

Holly read it. "Picture ID?"

He opened his briefcase and produced a well-stamped passport.

"A little travel tip," Holly said. "Don't ever carry your passport in a briefcase; it could be too easily stolen. Put it into an inside jacket pocket and button it down."

"Point taken," Schell said, doing as instructed.

"Have a seat," Holly said. "Coffee?"

"Thanks, I've already had mine," he replied, sitting down. "You don't want to know me on more than one cup of coffee."

"I understand you want to poke around the State Department for a while," she said.

"I promise not to do any poking. I just want to get a feel for the place, so I can get my readers to think they've been here before. Verisimilitude."

"A few rules," Holly said. "Don't open any desk or file drawers. Don't mess with anybody's computers. Don't hit on the women. If you ask somebody a question and don't get a straight answer, move on to another question. There are others, but I can't think of them right now. We haven't had a visitor like you before."

"I'm grateful for the opportunity, Madam Secretary, and I'll try not to infringe on anybody's good nature."

Holly flipped through his file. "I see you have all the clearances, so I won't take the trouble to bar you from any large meetings. Smaller, more intimate ones are another thing entirely. You'll need my or Mac's permission for those."

"If I stray too far afield, just give a sharp jerk on my leash, and I'll sit and stay."

"That's a start," she said. "This is Maclean McIntosh, deputy secretary. He's Mac, and I'm Holly."

"How do?" he said to Mac. "I'm Marty. Holly, can I ask you what your usual day is like?"

"I haven't had a usual day yet," Holly said. "It's a morass of meetings, phone calls—many of them to or from abroad, and many of them contentious. We try to be diplomatic, but it doesn't always work." She turned to McIntosh. "Mac, get this guy a badge, one of the good ones."

"Yes, ma'am." Mac left the room.

"You want to tell me what your book is about?" she asked.

"You already know what my business is here," Schell replied. "As for the book, let's just say it's about diplomacy, domestic and foreign."

Mac came back with a plastic-encased visitor's badge, green in color. It had Schell's photo, taken by the security staff, already on it. "Hang this around your neck," Mac said, handing it to Schell. "Don't take it off until you're out of the building, and don't forget to wear it tomorrow and every day you're with us. And give it back to me when you leave."

"Right," Schell replied.

Holly got up, walked to a door, and opened it. "This is a vacant secretary's office," she said. "You can camp here, but don't use the phones. Use your mobile."

"Right." Schell walked into the office and sat down.

"Did you bring a laptop?" she asked.

"In my briefcase," he replied.

"Keep it in your briefcase when you're here, but lock it in that cabinet if you don't want to haul it around." She pointed. "The key's in the center desk drawer."

He opened the drawer and found it. "Thanks."

"I'll leave you to it." She left the small office and closed the door behind her.

A few minutes later, there was a knock on the door she had just closed. "Come in."

Schell walked in. "I need a few minutes alone with you sometime today," he said.

"Now is good," she said. "Close the big door and sit down."

He did. "Let's start with the obvious: How long have you known Mac McIntosh, and what's his background?"

"About eight years, starting at the Agency. He came to the White House with me as chief of staff of the National Security Council, then to State when I moved over. He's a Boston boy: Exeter, followed by Harvard where he stayed long enough to get a PhD in poli-sci. Speaks three or four languages. Married, no kids."

"Do you think he might be a good fit for a mole?"

"I don't know what a good fit for a mole is," she replied.

"Have you ever learned anything about him that surprised you? Something not in his file?"

Holly thought about that. "He sings and plays folk and jazz guitar. We can't shut him up at parties."

"What's his wife like?"

"New Yorker, Harvard, like that. She works for the Joint Chiefs of Staff; I've no idea what she does there."

"Does she speak any languages?"

"Spanish, I think."

"Does either of them speak German or Russian?"

"Mac speaks both, though he says his Russian isn't so hot. Why do I think you've already read both their files?" Holly asked.

"I'm looking for stuff that isn't in their files," Schell replied. "Is there anybody on this floor that you regard as even a little suspicious? Furtive, takes a lot of work home, a linguist?"

"Nobody furtive, but lots of the other two."

"Is there a staff meeting scheduled for this week?"

Holly checked her calendar. "This afternoon at three, room 721, one floor down."

"Is that where the staff meeting was held when Mac spoke those words that got picked up on the GRU intercept?"

"Yes," Holly said. "And yes, it's been swept, no bugs present."

"See you there," Schell said, then left.

Stone was at his desk when his Agency iPhone went off. "Stone Barrington."

"Scramble." It was Holly.

"Scrambled."

"Hey."

"Hey, yourself. Are you back at State?"

"Yes, and I found Lance's guy waiting for me. I hope he solves this fast."

"What's your hurry?"

"I can't announce while this guy is still working."

"Everybody already knows you're running."

"Yeah, but if you're a federal employee and you decide to run for public office, you have to resign, unless you're the president or vice president running for reelection. I can't walk away from this job while this investigation is in progress."

"Why not? Leave it for the next secretary."

"So, I resign today and announce, and next month Marty Schell finds the mole in the State Department, and it's front-page stuff.

And the first news conference or debate question I get asked is, 'Why didn't you find the mole?' I don't want that hanging around my neck for the whole campaign."

Stone sucked his teeth. "No, you don't."

"Did you notice that I'm crying on your shoulder?"

"That's what shoulders are for," Stone said.

"I can make speeches on the subject of foreign policy, though, even if the Republicans say I'm campaigning on the federal dime. In fact, I'm speaking to the Foreign Policy Association next week, in New York, of all places."

"Fancy that!"

"I do," she said, "and there should be time to fancy you, as well."

"I'll have the sheets changed."

"Why would they need changing?" she asked, suspiciously.

"Just a matter of form, when a guest arrives."

"Or when one departs."

"Don't go there."

"I know, I know, I won't complain if you need a sex life when I'm not around."

"When you're around, too."

"But when I'm not, I can be jealous."

"Jealousy doesn't become you, but you have other qualities."

"Like breasts, you mean?"

"Of course and still other qualities. I'll point them out to you as soon as you arrive."

"Thanks, I'll need that. See you next week."

"Let me know your flight time, and Fred will meet you."

"I couldn't live without him. Bye." She hung up.

Lance called a few minutes later and scrambled.

"Good morning," Stone said.

"And to you. Our agent at State has arrived and is on the job."

"I'm glad to hear it. How will he investigate?"

"It's an easy start. There were thirty or so people in the staff meeting where the now all-too-familiar words were uttered. They'll all get a 701C review."

"What's a 701C?"

"The FBI's most thorough background check is called a 701. Our version is the 701C, and it's tougher."

"I'm not sure I'd want to undergo that," Stone said.

"You have already done so and passed, or I could not have installed you here as a deputy director."

"I guess that's a good thing, then."

"Except for the fact that I now know everything about you that's worth knowing."

"I have nothing to hide," Stone said.

"Not anymore," Lance replied. "I must say that I was impressed with the list of women. It goes all the way back to that thing in the back seat of a Buick parked on West Tenth Street, the summer before you entered NYU."

"Let's not go there," Stone said.

"I think the press would have a field day with that one, since the young lady in question is now the junior United States senator from New Jersey."

"I *said*, let's not go there."

"As you wish."

"Tell me, who else has access to my file besides you?"

"Oh, almost everybody."

"*What?*"

"Joking. Only a superior with a need to know may see the file, and you have only one superior."

"That's a relief."

"Of course, should I levitate to better things, you would have a new superior."

"In that event, can you put a blowtorch to it?"

"That would be destroying public property and against the law."

"Public property?"

"Perhaps *Agency* property would be a better way to put it. I suppose I could take it with me."

"It would be easier if, in that event, you just handed it to me."

"What would you do with it?"

"Maybe it could have an accident?"

"Files don't have accidents, people do."

"Who's to say?"

"We'll see," Lance said.

"Don't be coy, Lance. When I accepted the post, I hadn't counted on somebody digging into my private existence."

"Stone, it's just how the government works. It needs to know."

"I never thought of the government having needs," Stone said.

"You trust the government, don't you, Stone?"

"That depends on who's in charge of it."

"In this very limited case, I am. Tell you what, I'll send you the necessary codes for you to access your file, in the event of my death or ascension to a higher place. Once you've accessed it, you can delete it."

"Are there copies?"

"Oh, perhaps in a salt mine somewhere. Nobody ever goes down there."

"Promise?"

"I try never to make promises I can't keep."

Stone groaned. "Did you call just to ruin my day?"

"Well, your morning, perhaps," Lance said, chuckling.

"Unscramble," Stone said, and hung up.

J oan buzzed Stone. "There's a Callie Stevens, from Teterboro on the phone, line one."

Stone, thinking it had something to do with his airplane, punched the button. "Stone Barrington."

"This is Callie Stevens, of Wings at Teterboro. Can you have lunch with me at the Grill today?"

"What's this about, Ms. Stevens?"

"Your airplane. I'll explain everything at lunch, and I'm buying."

Stone had nothing on his schedule, and he was bored. "All right, what time?"

"Twelve-thirty?"

"See you then. How will I know you?"

"I'll know you," she said, then hung up.

Stone climbed the stairs into the Grill, formerly the Four Seasons. A woman at the bar left her stool and approached him. "Good afternoon," she said, "I'm Callie."

Callie was, perhaps, five-nine, a hundred thirty pounds, with honey-blond hair to her shoulders, and wearing an expensive-looking dress that revealed impressive cleavage. Stone shook her hand, and they were escorted to a table on the next level, where there was a bottle of Dom Pérignon awaiting them in an ice bucket on the table. A waiter opened it and poured for them.

"Well," Stone said, raising his glass, "this is a very nice start to lunch with someone I've never met. What's this about my airplane?"

Callie smiled. "I'm afraid it's growing less useful to you as we speak."

Stone frowned. "Termites?"

She laughed a pleasant laugh. "Lack of range, I'm afraid. And comfort."

"How so?"

"Well, let's say you want to fly to your home in the South of England," she said. "You'd have to stop at St. John's, Newfoundland, to refuel and, likely, to stay the night so your crew can rest. The following morning, you take off for England, but if you're just a little unlucky, the tailwinds are less than forecast, so you have to refuel at Shannon, in Ireland, before continuing to your private airfield."

Stone had to agree; he had had that experience more than once.

"Then there's the return trip. Against the wind you'd almost certainly have to stop at Shannon again, then St. John's, and you'd make Teterboro exhausted. It would take a couple of days to get over the jet lag."

"And how do you suggest I deal with that problem?"

"With an airplane that has twice the range as yours, that has a bedroom, and that cruises at five hundred knots. And it has bunks and a head for the crew up front."

"The perfect solution," Stone said as the waiter approached. "I'll have the Dover sole, pommes soufflées, and haricots verts."

"For two," Callie said to the waiter, and he disappeared.

"And how old is this airplane?" Stone asked.

"Less than two years, and it has just under six hundred hours on the clock."

"Doesn't the owner like it?"

"The owner, I fear, has no further use for it; he has left the planet, on a one-way ticket." She reached into her handbag and produced an iPad. "Have a look at the decor," she said. "Just touch the pictures you'd like to enlarge."

Stone went through the interior tour and found the layout and fabric and leather options to be very much what he would have chosen himself, if he had been ordering it new. "It's a Gulfstream 500," he said.

"You have a good eye," Callie replied. "It's loaded, too, with just about every avionics and entertainment choice you could ask for. And the rear cabin has a shower."

Stone continued to view the photographs.

"And," she said, swallowing a bite of her sole, "I can make the entire transaction happen by the close of business tomorrow."

They ordered coffee.

"How long has the owner been dead?"

"Since last summer. It's had about a hundred hours of charters since then."

"Did you steal the airplane?" Stone asked.

"No, but you can."

Stone laughed. "You're a broker?"

"I am. An independent. I spent eleven years with two of the biggest brokers in the business, was the top seller for both, and, when they wouldn't come up with a partnership, I went out on my own. I was able to persuade the late owner's estate to give me an exclusive on the airplane, and you're the first to see it."

"I haven't seen it," Stone said.

"My car is waiting outside. How about a test flight?"

"How did you choose me to be your first buyer?"

"I've seen you around," she said, "and I've talked to people. I've also run a Dun & Bradstreet report on you, and I'm aware that you and your investment partners have just made out like bandits on an initial public offering, so you can just write a check for the aircraft."

"How big a check are we talking about?" Stone asked.

"That will depend on your reaction when you see and fly the machine. Shall we go?" She signed the bill and stood up.

Stone followed her down the stairs to the street and into a '70s-vintage Bentley, which had been restored to like-new condition. Twenty-five minutes later they were walking around the airplane, while two uniformed pilots and a stewardess awaited their pleasure.

Stone climbed up the airstairs and entered the cabin. He was immediately impressed with the spaciousness. There were eight seats in two club arrangements. He checked out the owner's bedroom, toilet, and shower, then went forward and looked at the galley, the pilots' rest area, and then the cockpit.

"Take the left seat," Callie said, and the captain slid past her and into the right seat.

"You're going to let me fly this thing?" Stone asked.

She handed him a headset and the checklist. "Why not? You've had all but five hours of the required training over the past eighteen months, and Captain Jim, here, is a certified flying instructor at Gulfstream for this type."

"Where are we going?" Stone asked.

"Where would you like to go?" she replied.

"How about up to my house in Maine? We can land at Rockland."

"Perfect."

"Shall we stay the night? There's room for everybody."

"Your wish is our command," she said.

"Would you call my office and tell my secretary, whose name is Joan, that I'll be back sometime tomorrow, and to call the Rockland FBO and ask them to get my Cessna out of the hangar? Also, ask her to call the Maine house and let the staff know we're on the way, expect to land at Islesboro in two hours, and would like to dine at seven?"

"Of course," she said, disappearing into the cabin.

Stone was familiar with the cockpit and avionics from having flown more than twenty hours in the simulator at Gulfstream, in Savannah, Georgia, and he ran through the checklist and entered a flight plan into the computer, while Captain Jim got a weather report, filed the flight plan, and got a clearance.

"We got your requested routing," Captain Jim said. "I think you must have flown it before."

Stone nodded, then called ground control and got permission to taxi, and while they were waiting for release at the end of runway one, Captain Jim set up the auto throttles, and they ran through the takeoff checklist together. Then, cleared for takeoff, Stone guided the big airplane onto the runway with the tiller and advanced the throttles.

They reached rotation speed astonishingly quickly, and at five hundred feet, Stone switched on the autopilot. All he had to do now was watch the airplane fly itself.

They touched down a little less than an hour later at Rockland and taxied to the ramp, where Stone's Cessna 182 awaited. They transferred to the smaller airplane, and twenty minutes later they were landing on the 2,450-foot runway on Islesboro, a large island in Penobscot Bay, where Stone's caretaker, Seth Hotchkiss, awaited them in a 1938 Ford woodie station wagon. The crew tossed their overnight bags into the back.

Ten minutes later they were at Stone's place, and Seth was escorting the crew to the guesthouse.

While everyone was getting settled, Stone called his friend and client Mike Newman, CEO of Strategic Services, the world's second-largest security company and whose hangar space Stone's airplane shared.

"Where are you?" Mike asked.

"In Maine, coming home tomorrow. I'll be landing in a G-500 about noon; would you ask your flight management director and his people to go over the airplane and check out the logbooks?"

"I have already done so," Mike replied.

"What?"

"Callie Stevens called me a couple of days ago, and they finished their inspection this morning. Everything is triple-A perfect, the logbooks are up to date, and it's had all its inspections."

"If I buy it, can you squeeze it into your hangar?"

"Yes. Excuse me, Stone, I have to run to a meeting." Mike hung up.

Stone hung up, too, amazed.

They dined on lobster and a good Chardonnay, then the crew went to their rooms, and Stone and Callie sat down before the fireplace with their brandy.

She was very attractive, Stone thought, but they had business to do, and that would have to wait. They chatted about nothing in particular, and he was glad that she didn't keep selling.

Finally, he showed her up to a guest room, then went to his own and collapsed into bed. He had loved the flight up, and he had that familiar tingle when he was about to spend too much on something he wanted.

8

The following morning, after a good breakfast, they traveled back to the Rockland airport and took off for Teterboro. As soon as they had the gear up, Jim reached for the throttles and pulled them to the off position. "You've just lost an engine," he said. "Handle it."

Stone was ahead of him: he applied the opposite rudder, retrimmed the airplane, and got it settled down.

"Now, return to the airport and land," Jim said. "Hand-fly the approach; I'll handle the radios."

Stone contacted the tower and advised them of his return, then made left traffic while he loaded the instrument approach into the flight computer. He flew the airplane down to five hundred feet, on course and flight path, then Jim pushed the throttle forward. "You just got your engine back," he said. "Now climb to three thousand feet and reduce your speed to two hundred knots." He produced a clipboard and began taking notes. Then, when the aircraft had settled down, he switched off the autopilot and put Stone through the standard series of stalls. That done, he directed Stone to fly to Teterboro. Forty minutes later, as air traffic control gave them a descent, Jim listened to the automatic weather frequency. "The wind is 080 at twenty knots, gusting thirty," he said. "Hand-fly the ILS for runway six and put it on the center line." He switched off the autopilot again.

Stone flew the approach, crabbing into the strong wind to keep the airplane on the runway center line, set down softly on the right gear, then used the sidestick and ailerons to set down on the left. He turned off the runway and headed for Jet Aviation.

Stone taxied to the ramp, then ran through the checklist and shut everything down.

"I'm impressed with your skills," Jim said. "So I have a little gift for you." He handed Stone his clipboard. "I'm a certified FAA flight examiner, and you have just passed your check ride for your type rating in the G-500. Sign here." He pointed to an X. "And let me have your old license."

Stone signed. "What about my last five hours of training?"

"I'll sign you off for that," Jim said. "I'm still a part-time instructor for Gulfstream, and you've now completed all the requirements." He handed Stone the paper he had just signed. "This is your temporary license. Your old one goes back to the FAA; they will add your new type rating and send you a new license."

"Jim," Stone said, "is there anything wrong with this airplane that you know about?"

"No, sir. She just had a major inspection at Gulfstream, and everything is up to snuff."

"Are you happy with your copilot?"

"The kid is a good pilot, but he's young and single and comes to work too often with a hangover."

"I have a pilot on staff who's excellent. I'll ship her down to Gulfstream and let her get type-rated, then you can let the kid go."

"That sounds like a good plan."

"My pilot's name is Faith Barnacle. She's been in charge of my flight department, as well as flying. You two can work together on that."

"Sounds good," Jim said.

"Then I'd better go buy this airplane." Stone exited the cockpit and left the crew to do their work while he and Callie walked into the fixed-base operator and took a table in the pilots' lounge. "All right," he said, "what do you want for the airplane?"

She named a figure. "That's an attractive number," Stone replied, "but not quite low enough." He named a number.

She shrugged, then gave him another number. "That includes the trade-in on your Citation Latitude," she said. "I've already sold it." She wrote down the numbers and pushed a sales contract and a pen across the table.

Stone laughed, then he read the contract and signed it and a half dozen additional documents that covered maintenance and other minutiae, plus another sales contract for his airplane.

"Now all I need is a cashier's check," she said.

Stone picked up his phone and called Charley Fox, his partner, along with Mike Freeman, in Triangle Investments, which handled all his money.

"I hear you bought a new airplane," Charley said.

"Apparently, everybody in the northeastern United States knows that, but I just found out myself. Write down this number." He read it from the sales contract. "Bust into my investment account and generate a cashier's check in that amount, then have it hand delivered to . . ." He looked at Callie.

"Your office," she said. "I'll give you a ride in."

"My office," Stone said, "soonest."

"You'll have it inside an hour," Charley said, and they hung up.

"Now," Callie said, "I understand you already have a pilot on staff?"

"That's correct. I've told Jim about it. She'll have to go through the training, but I can fly with Jim until she's done."

"I suggest you hire the crew, Jim Stafford and his wife, Julie. They've been with the airplane since it was new."

"I have already done so. Jim isn't happy with his first officer, so he'll let him go as soon as Faith is back from Savannah."

"Right." She handed him some other documents. "These are Jim's and Julie's contracts, which include a ten percent raise over what the last owner was paying. Jim and Julie have a house near Teterboro, one kid in college. Jerry is single and lives in the city."

Stone signed the papers. "Anything else?"

"I assume you'll want to keep your tail number?"

"That is correct."

"I'll handle it with the FAA, and the change will be made tomorrow in the Strategic Services hangar."

"Good. Anything else?"

"Not a thing. Congratulations," Callie said, offering her hand.

Stone took it. "That was the slickest performance I've ever seen," he said.

"I've been working on it for a week," she replied. "You never had a chance of avoiding it."

They walked to her car and headed for Manhattan. Stone called Joan.

"Congratulations on the new airplane," she said.

"It's a conspiracy," Stone replied. "Please call Arthur Steele and get the new airplane on my policy and remove the old one. Make the hull value thirty million dollars, and the liability remains the same." He read her the aircraft and engine serial numbers off the sales contract, then hung up. He turned to Callie. "Lunch on me?"

"Can we make it dinner? I need to work with my other client on completing the sale of your Latitude."

"My house at seven?"

"Done."

"You're a wonder," he said.

"You have no idea," she replied.

Back at home, Stone handed Joan the paperwork for the airplane to be filed. Then he went to his desk.

Joan buzzed him immediately. "Dino on one."

Stone pressed the button. "Yeah?"

"Congratulations," Dino said.

"Jesus."

"I understand we can now fly nonstop to your house in England."

"That is correct."

"Have you flown it yet?"

"I flew it up to Islesboro yesterday and back this morning."

"When do we leave?"

"You're just dying to fly it somewhere, aren't you?"

"I am, and so is Viv."

"I'll call you tomorrow and let you know where."

"Gotcha." Dino hung up.

Joan buzzed. "Faith called, and I told her about the new airplane."

"She'll need to take the Gulfstream course and get a new type rating."

"We've already scheduled it, starting Monday," Joan said.

Stone hung up. "Jesus," he muttered to himself.

Callie showed up on time in another watchable dress. He took her into the study and made her a martini and himself a Knob Creek on the rocks. He handed her the cashier's check. "There you are," he said. "Nice dress."

"Thanks, you just paid for it, and the note on the Bentley, too."

"Will you have any money left?"

"Yes, that came from the new owner of your Latitude."

"I should have known."

"You know," she said, "dealing with so many wealthy people over the years, I've seen a lot of nice houses, but this is the most *comfortable* one I've been in."

"That's high praise. Thank you."

They sipped their drinks.

"Now," he said, "you know everything about me, except where I buy my underwear."

"Ralph Lauren outlet stores," she said. "Usually Vero Beach."

Stone laughed. "Sorry, I underestimated you. Now, it's time for you to tell me about you."

"I'm from a small town in Georgia called Delano. Went to the local schools and hung out at airports. I got a degree in aviation management at Embry-Riddle University, plus my license, instrument rating, and a few type ratings—turboprop and jet—then I flew corporate for a couple of years. One of my passengers offered me a job with his aircraft sales company, and the rest you already know."

"Never married?"

"Once, for about fifteen minutes, while I was at Embry-Riddle. That was enough. I'm a free woman."

"The very best kind," Stone said.

Fred came into the room and informed them that dinner would be served in ten minutes. Stone introduced him to Callie.

"How do you do, miss?" Fred said. "Mr. Barrington, congratulations on the new airplane."

"Thank you, Fred."

Fred disappeared, and ten minutes later began bringing in dishes.

They were on dessert when Callie put down her fork. "That was wonderful," she said.

"I'm glad."

"I can't wait to see your next move."

"Would you like to see the master suite?"

"Love to."

He poured them both a cognac, and they took their glasses and the elevator upstairs.

She invited him to unzip her, and she wasn't wearing a bra. She turned to give him a full view. "I'll bet you're a breast man," she said.

"The sight of breasts is good for morale," Stone replied.

"And they're original equipment," she said.

"Always to be admired, though I'm not picky about that sort of thing."

They snuggled in bed, and she fondled him. "This was the only thing I didn't know about you," she said, "but I guessed right."

He did some fondling of this own, then they got down to cases.

When Stone came out of the bathroom the following morning, Callie was sitting up in bed, with her beautiful breasts on display.

"What a wonderful sight," Stone said, kissing them. The dumb-waiter bell rang. "Excuse me, that's breakfast," he said.

She pulled up the covers.

"It's all right. Breakfast is arriving alone." He took the trays out of the lift and arranged them on the bed.

"How'd you know what I'd like?" she asked.

"I was feeling my way," Stone replied.

"I was referring to breakfast," she said, laughing.

"Who doesn't like scrambled eggs and sausage?"

"Nobody doesn't like that."

"Good. Would you like to fly somewhere with me tomorrow?"

"Sure. Where did you have in mind?"

"How about Paris?"

"I could be dragged there. I'll need to pack, of course."

"Travel light, and we'll shop. Oh, and some friends will be coming."

"Would that be Dino and Vivian Bacchetti?"

"I forgot, you know everything about me."

"I do now."

"They're good people. You'll like them."

"I'll look forward to it, then."

After breakfast, they made love again, then Callie excused herself. "I have to complete the sale of your airplane," she said.

"Give me your address, and we will call for you at eight in the morning. I'd like to be in Paris for dinner."

She handed him a card. "That's everything," she said, "all the numbers."

Stone gave her his card.

"Who does your overseas flight handling?" Callie asked.

"Pat Kramer," he replied.

"Excellent. We'll be in good hands." She bent over to kiss him, giving him yet another view. "See you tomorrow morning at eight."

Stone watched her go, then picked up the *Times* and switched on *Morning Joe*.

Stone had just reached his desk when Dino called.

"Good morning."

"Same to you."

"Where are we heading tomorrow?"

"How about Paris?"

"Great! Viv will love that. Who are you bringing?"

"The broker who sold me the airplane. Her name is Callie Stevens."

"I can't wait. What time?"

"Why don't you pick me up at seven-thirty. Then we'll get Callie and be off, arrive in time for dinner."

"Brasserie Lipp?"

"I'll have Joan book it."

"See ya." Dino hung up.

Stone buzzed Joan.

"Yes, sir?"

"Please book me for four at Brasserie Lipp, eight o'clock tomorrow night."

"You're going to try the new airplane, huh?"

"You betcha."

"Consider it done." She hung up.

10

They arrived at the Strategic Services hangar at Teterboro on time and were met by Captain Jim and his wife, Julie, plus the first officer.

"Anything you'd like in the cabin?" Jim asked.

"My briefcase."

"Mine, too," Dino said.

"Also mine," Viv added.

"Mine is in my hand," Callie said.

"You should speak to the service manager," Jim said.

Before Stone could respond, he heard an odd noise, like a basketball being dribbled very slowly, and turned to see the service manager coming toward him, bouncing a tire.

"Good morning, Mr. Barrington," the man said.

"Good morning, Dick. What have you got there?"

"One of your tires."

"Why isn't it on the airplane?" Stone asked.

Dick held up the tire in both hands. There was about a six-inch slit in the sidewall.

"That looks intentional," Stone said.

"That's how I read it, too. We've had airport security and the police over here, and they confirmed my diagnosis."

"Any idea when or how that happened?"

"In the middle of the night," Dick said. "That's the only time there was nobody here—from about eleven PM till about five this morning. Luckily, we had a new one in stock, and it's on your airplane, ready to go. We'll bill your account."

"How'd they get in?"

"Bolt cutters on a padlock. Nothing slick."

"Any suspects?"

"None. Everybody who works here likes you and was in bed, asleep."

"Good to know, on both counts."

"The cops will continue to work on it, they say, but I'm not expecting an imminent arrest."

"Then we'll get out of here," Stone said. "Thanks for your help, Dick." He turned and walked toward the airplane and noticed that his old tail number was already on it. "Fast work," he said to Callie.

"I know somebody at the FAA," she replied, "and somebody at the paint shop."

"Shall we go aboard?" He ushered the others ahead of him.

In the cabin, everybody oohed and aahed. "It's you," Viv said.

"I thought so, too," Stone replied, "the moment I saw it."

They all found seats facing one another.

"What made you spring for the dough?" Dino asked. "I mean, I knew you were crazy, but not *this* crazy."

"Well, Mike, Charley, and I made a bundle in that IPO, and I was feeling guilty about having so much cash, so I decided to become poorer."

"We did okay in the IPO, too," Dino said, "but not crazy good like this."

"I'm happy for you both."

"Me, too."

Julie approached. "Would anyone like a hot breakfast when we're at altitude?"

Everybody said yes.

"Excuse me for a few minutes," Stone said. He got up and walked to the cockpit, where Captain Jim waited in the right seat.

"I thought you might like to fly her to altitude," Jim said.

"You read me well." Stone slid into the left seat, strapped in, put on a headset, and reached for the checklist.

"I've already entered our clearance," Jim said.

"At what altitude?"

"Flight level 510. Okay?"

"Fifty-one thousand feet is better than okay."

Once again, Stone got the airplane off the runway, then watched the autopilot do the rest. He was talking to Jim and barely noticed when the aircraft leveled off at FL 510. Soon they were taking advantage of a 160 knot tailwind, bound for Le Bourget, doing 650 knots over the ground and soon over the sea.

"I think you'll make your dinner reservation," Jim said, "and have time for a drink first."

"Jim," Stone said, "have you ever had any vandalism problems with the airplane?"

"No," Jim said, "not a one, until today. Does somebody hate you?"

"Not this week that I'm aware of. How about you?"

Jim looked thoughtful and shook his head slowly.

"Anybody else on the crew have that problem?"

"No, but I guess it's natural for you to ask."

"I'm a former cop," Stone said, "and the guy in the back is the New York City police commissioner. We look, by instinct, for motive."

"I understand."

Julie leaned over from behind Stone's seat. "Mr. Barrington, are you ready for breakfast?"

"It's Stone, Julie—to all of you—and I certainly am." He released his five-way seat belt, got up, and rejoined the others, settling in next to Callie.

"You talk to your pilot about motives?" Dino asked.

Stone nodded.

"Nobody's after me," Dino said, "nor Viv—not that she'll tell me about, anyway."

"I guess that leaves me," Callie said.

"Anybody hate you?" Stone asked.

"Well, let's see," she said. "There's my competition, especially my former employers, but they're not nuts enough to do something like that. Anyway, they love airplanes, and they would never harm one on purpose."

"Anybody else?" Stone asked. "Ex-husbands, ex-lovers, rejected suitors, female competitors for men?"

"I ran through my mental checklist, and I couldn't come up with anything."

"How about your ex-husband?" Stone asked. He had had problems for years with a string of those.

"That was a long time ago," she said, "better than ten years."

"How long since you've seen him?"

"Maybe a year. He's an airline pilot, and I occasionally bump into him at airports. He's always cordial."

"Does he have a history of violence against others?"

"Only me that I'm aware of, but I gave as good as I got."

"Did he try to kill you?" Dino asked.

"If he did, he didn't try hard enough," Callie replied.

"Did he use a weapon on you?" Viv asked.

"We're all ex-cops here," Stone said, "except Dino, who's still on the job."

"He threw a glass of beer at my head and missed," Callie said. "If you can call that a weapon."

"A toothbrush is a weapon," Dino said, "and almost any other object, if you can swing it or throw it."

"I don't think anybody was trying to kill one of us," Stone said. "The cut wasn't meant to work on takeoff or landing. The tire was already flat when the shop opened early this morning."

"Maybe it was a warning," Dino said.

"Anybody have a response to that?" Stone asked the group.

Nobody did, and scrambled eggs and bacon were served.

A car met them at Le Bourget and drove them into the city to Saint-Germain-des-Prés. They stopped at a large set of oaken doors, and Stone dug out his remote control from a pocket. The doors swung open to reveal an ancient mews that contained Stone's house, which had once been owned by the CIA and used as a safe house. He had bought it from them, at a very good price, when the government adopted a policy of unloading excess real estate everywhere.

Marie, the housekeeper, caretaker, and cook, greeted them at the door in a flood of French, in which Stone could barely tread water, and everyone went to their assigned quarters.

"This is lovely," Callie said. "I can't wait to see your other houses. Why so many?"

"It's an affliction," Stone replied. "I see a house I like, and I want to buy it."

Showered, changed, and refreshed, they walked down the Boulevard St. Germain to Brasserie Lipp, a restaurant that, to Stone, was the Paris equivalent of Elaine's, his New York hangout for years, except that the cuisine was Alsatian and the clientele Parisian. On Stone's advice, they all ordered the choucroute garnie, a platter of sliced meats over sauerkraut, accompanied by large glasses of beer.

"I've been thinking about this morning's sabotage," Dino said.

"So have I," Stone replied. "Any conclusions?"

"Forgive me for saying so, Callie, but I think it's something to do with your presence in Stone's life, and probably Stone's fault."

"Have I done something to somebody?" Stone asked plaintively.

"Maybe you stole somebody's girl," Dino replied.

"And that would be me," Callie said.

"Unless Stone has another one concealed in his luggage," Dino pointed out.

"Okay," she said, "I'm willing for my ex to be the chief suspect for now, but I don't know how anybody is going to prove it."

"What's his name?" Dino asked.

"Eddie Casey."

"Full name?"

"Edward Woodward Casey."

"Got it," Dino said, and abandoned his choucroute long enough to send an e-mail.

"You met him in college?"

"Long before that; we're from the same hometown. He was a year ahead of me in school, and we dated for, maybe, three years."

"Do you know whether he has a criminal record?" Stone asked.

"Well, I charged him with assault and battery and domestic violence," Callie replied, "and he pled guilty and got a six-month sentence, suspended."

"How long was it before you saw him again?"

"He stopped by my place about a year later to apologize. He'd gotten into AA, and they're supposed to apologize to those they've hurt as a part of the program."

"Was he convincing?"

"Completely," she said. "I hadn't figured out how bad his drinking problem was, but he seemed to be a changed man. I didn't like the new guy all that much, either."

"How did he hang on to his pilot's license?" Viv asked.

"He never had a DUI, so there was nothing in his record indicating a drinking problem."

"It's been a long time since I filled out an application for a license," Stone said, "but I suspect there might have been a question that covered more ground than a DUI."

"You mean like, 'Did you ever get drunk and beat up your wife?'"

"Something like that."

"Well, he got his license a couple of years before the incident, so I guess he didn't feel a need to report it to the FAA, or he'd never have gotten a job flying."

"What sort of flying did he do after Embry-Riddle?" Stone asked.

"Package delivery, air charter, corporate—the usual for a new pilot looking to build time."

Dino's phone buzzed, and he looked at it. "Well, he still doesn't have a DUI," he said, "but he did get into a bar fight a couple of times, so he has an arrest record, but he was never charged. Also, he's not working for the airlines now; he's with one of those shared aircraft ownership outfits, based at—wait for it—Teterboro."

"Motive: Callie," Stone said. "Means: available at any hardware store. Opportunity: on the way to or from work. He's a good suspect."

Callie shrugged. "If you say so."

"The odds say so," Dino replied.

olly was at her desk when Mac knocked and entered.

"You look like a man with news," she said.

"I am, and from the Agency. There's good and bad: the good news is that everybody who was in the conference room that day has passed the Agency's 701C, and without breaking a sweat."

"And the bad news?"

"The same as the good news. We're back to square one."

"Mac, you remember when we had all those cameras installed last year?"

"Yep?"

"Was the big conference room one of the places they were installed?"

"Yep."

"Then why don't you go down to the basement to that little room where our paid wretches spend their days and nights doing the soul-destroying work of watching all those screens, and have them rewind to the day of that meeting and view the tapes from that day thoroughly."

"What will I be looking for or at?"

"You'll be looking at all of the people who attended that meeting, and for the least sign of furtiveness or odd behavior among them."

Mac sighed. "Yes, ma'am."

"I know, I know, but it has to be you, because you're the smartest guy in the building and the most observant. You'll know what to look for, and you'll know it when you see it."

"Yes, ma'am," Mac said and shuffled out.

Holly looked at her watch: well after breakfast time in Paris. She dialed the number on her personal cell phone.

Stone was sitting in a comfortable chair in his living room, doing the *Times* crossword and working on shedding his jet lag, while the others went for a bracing walk, when his iPhone rang.

"Yes?"

"Scramble."

"Scrambled."

"Good morning," she said.

"And good morning to you. How's life?"

"Tolerable."

"Any progress on the mole?"

"Well, we've eliminated all the good guys as suspects," she replied. "By the way, I hope I'm not infringing on your sex life."

"You can't have sex in an armchair while doing the *Times* crossword," he said. "Well, you could, I guess, but it wouldn't be much fun."

"I've never known you to be unable to find a suitable location and partner for that activity," she said, getting an affirmative grunt in response.

"How's the campaign going?"

"What campaign? I'm stuck until we find, or kill, the fucking mole. My campaign people are going nuts over my indecision. I can tell them they have to be patient, but I can't tell them why."

"There are already half a dozen people on the campaign trail," Stone said, "according to the part of my newspaper without a crossword."

"I read the same newspaper," she said, "and I get the same news on TV."

"Well, the news here is unintelligible, unless it's CNN, and they broadcast about the same twelve minutes over and over."

"How's the new airplane?" she asked.

"Jesus, you, too? I think everybody I know knew about it before I bought it."

"It must be very comfortable."

"It has a bed in the aft cabin. I'll show it to you sometime."

"No phone sex," she said, "not even scrambled. Hang on." She covered the phone for a few seconds, then came back. "Excuse me, but there's a fire somewhere to be put out. Later." She hung up.

It was a good thing there had been no phone sex, Stone thought, because Marie had gone grocery shopping and there was someone hammering on the front door. Stone got up and answered it.

Rick La Rose was standing at the door, and it was raining outside. Stone hadn't noticed. "Come in, Rick," he said. "Have you had breakfast?"

Rick was the Paris station chief for the Agency. "Yes, but I could use some coffee."

Stone headed for the kitchen. "What would you like in it?"

"Brandy, normally, but not at this time of day. Usually."

Stone returned with two mugs and handed one to Rick. "Come sit down."

They sat and sipped. "How'd you know I was here?" Stone asked. "This place isn't still wired for sound, is it?"

"I'm not prepared to comment on that," Rick said. "But an alarm did go off last evening when the gates were opened electronically, so I thought I'd see if you had a burglar."

"You folks have a very poor response time," Stone said.

"Yeah, but we always get around to it, eventually."

"'Eventually' isn't a response time. It's an excuse."

"It'll have to do," Rick said. "How's the new airplane?"

Stone sighed. "It's just wonderful, thanks. I flew it part of the way across the Atlantic yesterday."

"I didn't know you were type-rated in a G-500."

"I wasn't, until a couple of days ago. I've been doing a week or two at a time in the simulator for the past eighteen months. It adds up."

"I hear you had a little vandalism at Teterboro," Rick said.

"My life is an open book," Stone replied.

"Any suspects?"

"One, but we haven't got anything on him yet. I don't suppose that, with your general omniscience, you could finger somebody for me?"

"Her ex looks good for it," Rick said, "but who knows?"

"Maybe she knows, but if she does, she's not telling."

"That lady knows almost as much about you as I do," Rick said.

"That is irritatingly true," Stone said. "She knew where I buy my underwear."

"The Ralph Lauren outlet store? Who knew you were so cheap, Stone?"

"Why don't you and Lance get together with Callie and write my autobiography?"

"It's already in your file at Langley," Rick said, "and I don't think it would sell, because nobody would believe it."

"I'll try to live a more interesting life," Stone said, wryly.

"You're doing just fine, Stone," Rick said, then he stood up. "Thanks for the coffee. I'll see you around."

"I'll just bet you will," Stone said, showing him out.

13

Everyone gathered for drinks at six-thirty, perhaps a little damp from the afternoon rain, then Stone and Dino pulled the cover off the 1970s Mercedes, which had less than ten thousand miles on the odometer. With the top down, they drove over to Avenue Franklin Roosevelt, to the restaurant Lasserre—a haven of haute cuisine and old-school formality, where the male guests voluntarily wore neckties and the women could wear haute couture and their best jewelry without being stared at, because the other women were dressed that way, too.

They dined slowly, savoring the experience, all the while being attended by a squad of waiters wearing tails. The pianist played the old songs, and the ceiling periodically and silently opened to let out the hot air and to expose the rose arbor on the roof.

"I love coming back to this place," Dino said, uncharacteristically.

"I recall you being uncomfortable here," Stone replied, "on your first visit."

"That's because I didn't know what to expect," Dino said. "I thought it might be a French movie set, and that at any moment, a big camera and a crew would glide past the table."

"It's my first time here," Callie said, "and I love it." She took a sip of her claret. "I didn't know about the bar fights, Dino."

Dino managed to return to the present. "Bar fights?"

"The ones you said Eddie had been arrested for."

"Oh, *those* bar fights."

"That was just guy stuff, wasn't it? Harmless big-boy tiffs?"

"Not exactly," Dino replied. "You see, those bar fights happened in the sort of bars where people go looking for bar fights, the kind of place where there are baseball bats behind the bar, so the bartenders don't get hurt."

"Are you saying that Eddie hung out in such places all the time?"

"No, just the two times he got arrested for it. Of course, the second time is the clue. After getting arrested the first time, why did he go back for more?"

"Did he?"

"At least once. My guess is that he had visited such places more than once or twice before and, perhaps, after the arrests."

"Why would a person do that?"

"There are some persons who enjoy inflicting pain on others, and others who enjoy having it inflicted upon themselves."

Stone spoke up. "When Eddie decided to beat you up, which group do you think he belonged to?"

"Not *my* group," she said. "I just defended myself."

"Callie," Stone said gently, "there are certain traits in a suspect that a police officer looks for when making judgments about them. If, for instance, an arrestee has in his record a history of harming small animals—like household pets—alarms go off in his head and red lights flash, because that is a marker for a serial killer."

"I don't think Eddie did *that*," she said.

"And if the officer is investigating the murder of a woman, and her husband has a history of violence against women, then he becomes, at once, the chief suspect."

"Eddie wasn't trying to murder me," she said.

"Maybe next time," Stone replied. "You did the right thing when you got out immediately."

"I remember when we were in high school Eddie's father used to beat up his mother. The cops got called a couple of times."

"That's more history. Tell me, did you know other girls who dated Eddie?"

"There weren't any. We were going steady from the time I was fifteen. But he did get into fights playing football or basketball. He got thrown out of some games."

"Did Eddie ever suspect or accuse you of going out with other fellows?"

"Not exactly, but he did accuse me of being attracted to my avionics professor in college."

"Were you?"

"Attracted to him? Sure, he was cute."

"Did anything bad ever happen to your professor around that time?"

She looked down at her plate. "Somebody slashed the tires on his car once."

"It's a short hop from a car to an airplane," Stone said. "Around that time did Eddie ever rough you up?"

"He slapped me when I denied having anything to do with the professor."

Dessert came, and they fell upon it.

After dinner, the valet brought the convertible, and they took a midnight ride around Paris, talking little. Later, when they were getting ready for bed, Stone felt he had to bring up the subject of Eddie again.

"Callie?"

"Yes?" She was brushing out her hair at the dressing table.

"I think it's likely that you're going to see Eddie again."

"I don't want to see him."

"That won't stop him from trying."

"He got a broken nose the last time he took a swing at me."

"Eddie isn't a college boy anymore," Stone pointed out. "He has graduated to bigger things, like bar fights. Next time, he'll bring a weapon."

"Eddie never carried guns."

"Not that kind of weapon: a wine bottle, a broom handle, a kitchen knife. Whatever's handy."

"Why do you think he'll come after me?" she asked, looking at him in the mirror.

"Well, let's see," Stone said. "You saw him at an airport a year ago?"

"Less than a year. More like seven or eight months."

"How long ago did you leave your job and start your own company?"

"Two months ago."

"Was there an announcement in the aviation trade press?"

"Yes, I hired a PR lady to help me make a splash."

"Was it after that when Eddie left his airline job?"

"I'm not sure. Maybe."

"When he did, did he go to work for a company based at Teterboro—where you had recently opened offices?"

"Yes, he did. There was a piece on the *Aviation Week* website about my sale of the G-500 to you. The next day."

"Does he know where you live?"

"I don't think so."

"If he wanted to know, could he find out?"

"Maybe."

"Callie, I think you're being stalked. Do you own a gun?"

"No."

"Are you familiar with firearms?"

"Yes, I used to hunt with my dad. Shotguns."

"When we get back, I think you should take a weapons course—personal defense—and then I think you should buy a gun and keep it with you at all times. Dino will help with getting you a carry license."

"I don't like that idea," she said. "Maybe I could carry a blackjack?"

"That's an illegal weapon."

She was quiet for a moment. "All right," she said finally. "I'll take the course."

14

The next day, Stone arranged a car and driver for the women, then he and Dino went shopping at Charvet. Stone was greeted like an old customer, and he was told that his suit was ready for a final fitting. He had forgotten that he had ordered a suit and had fittings on subsequent visits to Paris.

The suit was nearly perfect, and before the day was out, it would be so. Dino took a deep breath and bought a cashmere dressing gown, while swearing that he would never wear it.

As he was waiting for Dino, Stone called his good friend Marcel du Bois, whose sobriquet was "France's Warren Buffett."

"Stone! How good to hear from you! I hear you bought a new airplane. Have you flown it to Paris?"

"Yes, Marcel. I'm at Charvet at the moment, for a fitting. Dino and Viv are traveling with me, as is a young lady."

"But of course!" Marcel said. "Will you all come to dinner at my home in the Bois this evening?"

"We'd be delighted."

"Six-thirty for drinks. Black tie, if you please."

"We please," Stone replied.

"What is your lady's name?"

"Callie Stevens."

"For the place cards. Good!" Marcel hung up.

"Marcel has invited us to dinner tonight at his home in the Bois de Boulogne. You'll get to wear your tuxedo."

Dino slapped his forehead. "I forgot to pack it."

"Back upstairs with you," Stone said. They went up and asked them to find Dino a dinner suit.

"I'm sorry, Mr. Barrington," the man said, "but we have dinner suits only to order. Is the suit for you?"

"No, it's for my friend Mr. Bacchetti here."

The man whipped out a tape measure and did some quick work on Dino. "I think, perhaps, I may have something," he said. He disappeared into a back room and, after a short wait, returned with a hanging bag and unzipped it. "This was made for a client who never took delivery," he said. "Would you slip into the jacket, Mr. Bacchetti?"

Dino did so, and it fit rather well. He tried on the trousers and the waistcoat, as well.

The man nodded his approval. "The sleeves and trousers will need a bit of shortening, and there's a wrinkle at the neck. I think we can make it work. Given the circumstances, I think we can offer you a substantial discount," he said.

"What are the circumstances?" Dino asked.

"An early death," he replied. "It was an accident . . . we are told."

"He'll take it," Stone said. Dino stood still for marking, then got back into his own clothes. The man promised to deliver it with Dino's dressing gown and Stone's suit to his house by five o'clock. Dino picked out a black bow tie.

"Do you have black shoes?" Stone asked Dino as they left the shop. He was wearing scuffed brown loafers.

"Not exactly," Dino said.

"Come with me." They took a cab to Berluti, where Dino was shod with the correct footwear. Dino gave the man a credit card, then said, "Jesus, I don't have any black socks!"

Stone sighed. "I'll loan you a pair. Call Viv and tell her about dinner, so she and Callie can find something spectacular to wear. Tell her it's at Marcel's and dress to kill."

Dino did so.

While Dino's shoes were being wrapped, Rick La Rose walked into the shop and greeted them. "Where are you bound?" he asked.

"To my house."

"I'll give you a lift while we talk."

"Talk?" Stone asked. This was not a good sign.

Ensconced in his armored black SUV, Rick got to the point. "There'll be someone at your dinner tonight that Lance wants to know more about."

"Dinner?"

"At Marcel du Bois's Bois house."

"Rick, is my phone tapped?"

Rick dismissed that with a wave of the hand. "He's an American, name of Peter Grant, who has lived in Paris for many years and could convince most Frenchmen that he's French."

"What does he do?"

"If you asked him that, he would say he's an investor. We don't know much more than that. Marcel, though, has invited the man to dinner."

"May I remind you, Rick, that Marcel invited you to dinner

once without having set eyes on you and having no idea who you were?"

Rick ignored that. "If he doesn't know Grant well, he'll want to. And the man is more likely to talk to him than to you."

"Do you have a list of questions for me to ask him?"

"Just anything and everything you can find out—from the other guests, too."

Stone turned to Dino. "This is what it's like to be a spy."

"Is that what you are?" Dino asked.

"Sometimes."

They arrived back at Stone's house in time for tea and a snack that would keep them going until dinner.

The women returned ladened with boxes and shopping bags.

"We both found something special for dinner tonight," Viv said.

"I was afraid of that," Dino said. "Is it going to be modeled for us?"

"You'll see it at dinner," Viv replied.

"You, too," Callie said to Stone.

They were in the convertible and on their way to the Bois de Boulogne when Stone had a thought. "Callie, do you know a man named Peter Grant?"

"Yes," she replied.

"No kidding? Do you know him well?"

"A lot better than I know you. Though I don't know where he shops for underwear."

"Tell me about him."

"What about him?"

"Tell me everything."

"How long is our drive?"

"Another ten minutes."

"Okay, I'll give you the ten-minute version," she said, and started to talk. "Born fifty-nine years ago in Boston—Southie, to be exact—not the best side of the tracks. Claims to have attended Groton and Harvard and to have been a Rhodes scholar, studying at Oxford. Moved to Paris as a young man and worked briefly at the *Paris Review*. Inherited some money, allegedly from a grandfather, and traveled widely in France, buying a house in Cap d'Antibes and an apartment in Paris, back when those were a lot cheaper. He was attractive to many women. Widely known in social circles in Paris and the Côte d'Azur, always a good spare man for dinner. Has his clothes made at Charvet in Paris and Huntsman in London. Rumor has it he has not returned to the United States since arriving in Paris all those years ago."

"That's all the time we have," Stone said, turning into Marcel's drive.

"Good, because that's all Peter has told me. By the way," Callie said, "almost none of this is substantiated. Grant may have invented everything I've just said."

They were received in Marcel's home in his usual high style—butler at the door, uniformed maids to take the coats, the best champagne in Baccarat flutes served from old silver trays, delicious canapés.

Marcel broke from a group, embraced Stone, and greeted everyone warmly. "It is so good to see you," Marcel said to Stone.

"That's because you come to New York so infrequently," Stone said. "And you haven't been back to my house in England since your first brief visit when we bought the adjoining property for an Arrington hotel."

"You are sadly correct, my friend. Paris always has such a grip on me. Everywhere else I am a foreigner."

"That's not such a bad thing to be," Stone said. Across the drawing room he caught sight of a man who might be his assignment for the evening. "Marcel, who is the gentleman standing next to the large sculpture?"

"Oh, that is Peter Grant. Do you know him?"

"I know some people who do," Stone replied.

"I'm afraid I don't know him very well. He's something in finance, independent, I'm told. He's charming company, good at evenings like this. Would you like to meet him?"

"I'll drift that way," Stone said. Then added, "When you have an opportunity you can introduce us."

"As you wish. I'll mingle, as is my duty as host." Marcel reached for another guest.

"So that's your guy?" Dino asked. "Would you like me to run him through our databases?"

"When you get a chance," Stone said. He took Callie's hand, and they began meeting people, with Dino and Viv close behind. Dino was staring at his iPhone.

Callie saw someone she had once sold an airplane to and introduced Stone, whose attention was elsewhere. Stone snagged them a fresh glass of champagne, then let the current take him toward Peter Grant. The man appeared to be a couple of inches taller than Stone, something that always annoyed him about a man. A beautiful redhead in a long black dress clung to his arm.

As Stone got closer, Marcel appeared and pressed him forward. "Peter," he said, "may I present my dear friend, Stone Barrington, and his friend Callie Stevens? Stone, this is Peter Grant and . . ."

"Tessa Martindale," the woman said, offering her hand.

Stone shook both hers and Grant's. "How do you do?" he asked.

"Very well," they answered simultaneously.

"Peter is in . . ." Marcel began. "What is it, Peter?"

"I invest," the man replied. "And you, Mr. Barrington?"

"I'm an attorney, and I serve on a couple of boards," Stone replied.

"With what firm?"

"I'm a senior partner at Woodman & Weld, in New York."

"Ah, yes," Grant replied with a slight frown.

"Oh, have we sued you?" Stone asked.

"Not yet," Grant said with a small smile.

"Peter never holds still long enough for anyone to sue him," Tessa said.

"A good policy," Stone replied. "In what do you invest, Peter?"

"Almost anything, if I can get a little inside knowledge."

"Then you had better worry more about being arrested than sued."

"I make it a point of never crossing the line of legality; it's too much trouble. A whisper at a party such as this is better than a glimpse of a confidential report on earnings."

"An interesting way to make a living," Stone said.

"Oh, I do a great deal more than that."

Cocky son of a bitch, Stone thought.

Dinner was announced, and Stone found himself seated between Tessa and a French dowager, while Callie was between Peter Grant and a man who could have been the dowager's brother.

"Do you live in Paris?" Stone asked Tessa, after seating her.

"Paris, London, and Cap d'Antibes," she replied. "Peter is a neighbor down there. And where do you live, Mr. Barrington?"

"It's Stone, please. New York, Los Angeles, Paris, and the South of England." He left out Key West and London.

"Where in the South of England?"

"Near Beaulieu, on the river."

"How lovely, if you can stand the weather."

"I love the weather. It was what drew me to England."

"Then you must have a bit of duck in you."

"Perhaps a bit. How long have you known Peter Grant?"

"Since I moved into his neighborhood in Cap d'Antibes a couple of years ago."

"How firmly attached are you to him?"

"A bold question."

"Being bold saves time."

"Then the answer is not very. We're both pretty slippery. How about you and Ms. Stevens?"

"We met only a few days ago. A business transaction."

"Ah, good."

"Do you work, or did you just choose the right ancestors?"

"A bit of both," she said. "I arrange events and parties, when I can summon the clients and the energy."

"Do you arrange events for Peter Grant?"

"Peter, I fear, is more often a guest than a host."

"How ungenerous of him."

"He is just a tiny bit tightfisted," she said. "Not a quality I admire in a man."

Stone wondered if that was a hint. "Nor a woman," he said.

She laughed. "I take it you're not referring to money."

"No."

"Then I am not ungenerous."

"Do you ever come to New York?"

"From time to time."

Stone gave her his card. "I'm in Paris for only a short time. Let me know if you fly across the pond."

"I'll do that," Tessa replied.

"Tell me, does Peter Grant own an airplane?"

"I think he relies on the kindness of those who do. Why do you ask?"

"Because the woman sitting next to him is trying very hard to sell him one."

"Then good luck to her," Tessa said.

T hey had just been served the main course when Stone saw Callie take her phone from her purse, look at it, then leave the table and the dining room. A couple of minutes later she stuck her head back inside, caught Stone's eye, and beckoned to him.

Stone excused himself and walked out into the hall. "Anything wrong?"

"Far from it," she said. "I've just learned I'm being considered to mark a Global Express 6000."

This was a much bigger and more expensive airplane than Stone's. "Congratulations," he said.

"Problem is, it's at Le Bourget, and it's leaving for New York in two hours."

"I'll take you . . ."

She held up a hand. "Don't leave the party. The butler has summoned a car for me. I'll go back to your house, pack, and be driven to Le Bourget. I'll be back in New York in time for a breakfast meeting with the seller's representative."

"As you wish," Stone said.

She kissed him and ran for the door, which was being held open by the butler.

Stone returned to the dining room and sat down.

"Problems?" Tessa asked.

"No, not at all."

"Is she coming back?"

"No, she's on her way to Le Bourget to catch a private flight to New York. She sells airplanes, and is being considered to sell a very expensive one, so she has to meet with the prospect tomorrow morning."

"My goodness," Tessa said. "That leaves you all alone, doesn't it?"

"Not quite," Stone said. "I have houseguests; would you like to join us for dinner tomorrow evening?"

"May I meet you somewhere?"

"My Paris address is on my card. Seven o'clock for drinks? We'll go on from there."

"Love to," she said.

After dinner the group moved into the library for cognac and coffee. Dino sat down beside Stone. "I ran a check on your mystery man."

"What did you find?"

"Zip. He's still a mystery. I couldn't even prove that he exists."

Stone glanced across the room at Peter Grant, who was sipping a liqueur from a small glass. "Do you still have contacts in the Paris police?"

"I do."

Stone rose. "I'll see you in a few minutes."

Dino tugged at his sleeve. "Where's Callie?"

"On her way to New York. I'll tell you about it later."

As Stone crossed the room, he saw Grant drain his glass and set it on the table beside him. It was swiftly taken away by the butler, set on a tray, and taken to the bar. Stone changed course and headed there. He finished his cognac and set down his glass.

"May I serve you more cognac?" the bartender asked.

"Please, a small one," Stone replied. While the bartender tended, Stone moved so that his body was between the tray of empties and the others in the room. He slipped Grant's glass into his jacket pocket and turned back in time to receive his new cognac.

Marcel arrived at Stone's side. "Your lady friend seems to have abandoned us," he said.

"She apologizes, Marcel, but she had to return to New York on short notice. Your butler was kind enough to provide a car to drive her to my house to pack and then to Le Bourget, where an airplane awaits her."

"Does she have something to do with airplanes?" Marcel asked.

"She does. Did she try to sell you one?"

"Somehow, the subject came up."

Stone laughed. "I hope you told her you already have a G-600."

"I did, and she told me that you just bought a G-500."

"I have," Stone said. "We flew it over."

"You will be very pleased with it, if your experience is anything like mine," Marcel said.

"Marcel," Stone said, "when your staff does a count of your crystal, they will find themselves one liqueur glass short."

"Did someone break one?"

"No, I borrowed a small one, for nefarious purposes. I will see that it is returned to you in a day or two."

"Well," Marcel said, "as long as your purposes are nefarious."

On the way home in the car, Stone took the glass from his pocket and handed it to Dino by the stem. "I swiped Peter Grant's glass," he said. "Will you see if one of your French cops can run prints and DNA on it?"

Dino produced a plastic bag from an inside pocket, deposited the glass in it, and made it disappear.

"Stone," Viv said from the back seat, "are you aware that Callie is not in the car?"

"I am," Stone said.

"Did she get a better offer?"

"No, just a bigger airplane to sell. She's on her way back to New York."

"You poor thing. Who will you play with?"

"Tessa Martindale, for dinner."

"I should have known," Dino said. "It's an assembly line."

The following morning, at a more decent hour than Stone would have expected, Lance Cabot called, then scrambled.

"How was dinner last evening?" Lance asked.

"You can imagine."

"I don't have to imagine, I had someone there."

"Rick La Rose must have been very well disguised," Stone said.

Lance ignored that. "What do you have on Peter Grant?"

Stone told him what he had been told.

"I know all that," Lance said. "I want something fresh."

"All right, as far as anyone knows he hasn't been back to the States in more than twenty-five years, and he's never had a driver's license in any state. That's as fresh as I've got, but I've taken another step that might bear fruit soon."

"You're just dangling me," Lance said.

"When I know, you'll know."

"The man is hiding something."

"If you can tell me what it is, then I might be able to make more headway."

"If I knew what it was, I'd tell you. You be in touch." Lance hung up.

Dino joined Stone for breakfast. "They sent a messenger over for the glass and hope to know something later today."

"That's good. Lance has already been on the phone this morning."

"Why is he so hot to trot on this guy?"

"Who knows? Lance's motives are always obscure. It may be in the line of work. It may be that Grant bullied Lance on a school-yard playground forty years ago. Also, Lance believes to his core that he needs and has a right to know everything about everybody who interests him, no matter what the reason."

"I feel that way sometimes myself," Dino said, "and so do you. About women."

"I'm okay with the bare bones," Stone said, "so to speak. I always figure the gaps will get filled in as we move along."

"But you so rarely move along that you never find more than the bare bones."

"Lance had somebody at the dinner last night, and it wasn't Rick La Rose."

"It was Tessa," Dino said. "I checked out the joint pretty well, and she's just what Lance would like in a spy."

"No, it wasn't Tessa. She's known Peter Grant for a couple of years, so if she's Lance's, he already knows what she knows. Who's your second choice?"

"I don't have one," Dino said. "I stopped when I got to Tessa."

"Yes, I know how you feel. She stopped me, too, and I forgot to thank Marcel for seating me next to her. I'll write him a note."

Stone put down his fork, took his coffee cup with him, went to the desk, and wrote Marcel a note. He signed it, sealed it, and left it for Marie to stamp and post.

"Your mother would be proud of you," Dino said, taking an armchair.

"She would at that."

"How much do you think a dinner party like that cost Marcel?" Dino asked.

"I don't know. Five hundred a head, maybe, but probably closer to a thousand, given the wines we drank."

"I never serve a guest anything that doesn't have a screw top," Dino said.

"The good news is: better wines are now being sold that way because they're running out of cork, but the prices of wines are not coming down."

"You know, the only old wines I've ever drunk have been at Marcel's house and your house."

"That's because most of the old wines I have were gifts from Marcel. He sends me a couple of cases a year."

The phone rang, and Stone picked it up. "Hello?" A voice asked for Dino in French. *"Un moment,"* Stone said, momentarily exhausting his French. He handed the phone to Dino. "It's for you."

"Hello?" Dino listened for about two minutes. *"Merci beaucoup,"* he replied and hung up. "That was fast," he said.

"What was fast?"

"That was my contact at the gendarme shop. They ran the prints on the glass, including yours, and the DNA and came up with a big, fat *goose egg.*"

Stone wondered what the French for goose egg was. "Nothing at all?"

"Oh, there was something," Dino said, raising a finger.

"Good."

"Grant got a speeding ticket on the Grand Corniche last year." The Grand Corniche was a famous stretch of winding road along the Côte d'Azur that fast drivers loved.

"Good to know," Stone said. "I'll pass that along to Lance first chance I get."

"Well, at least we know he has a French driver's license."

"Or one that the French would accept. They probably have a euro license by now, who knows?"

The doorbell rang. Marie answered it and brought a small package to Dino. *"Pour vous, m'sieur,"* she said.

Dino opened it and handed Stone Marcel's glass. "I know you'll want to return that." He also handed Stone a letter. "I think this says they came up with zilch, but here are Peter Grant's addresses in Paris and the Cap d'Antibes."

Stone stumbled through the French. "I think this is about the speeding ticket," he said. Slipping the letter into his pocket, he picked up his phone, called Lance, and scrambled.

"I've got something for you," he said. "Peter Grant had a speeding ticket on the Grand Corniche last year."

"Go on," Lance said.

"That's it. The only proof that the man exists on the planet, as far as I can tell."

"That's very disappointing, Stone."

"Lance, how is it you can tell me who I screwed in the back seat of a Buick twenty-five years ago, but you know fuck-all about Peter Grant?"

"You are a more visible subject," Lance said.

"Come to think of it, I believe I know why you can't learn anything about this man."

"Why is that?"

"Because he doesn't exist."

"Of course he exists," Lance said. "You had dinner with him last night."

"I mean, he doesn't exist by that name, except maybe in Paris, and I doubt there's any written record of him. Here's something you can check," Stone said, retrieving the letter to Dino and reading Lance the two addresses. "Get Rick La Rose to check the real-estate records of the addresses and find out who the owners of record are."

"Well, it's lame, but it's something."

"Here's something else for you," Stone said. "Check every county clerk's records in the United States and see if there was an application for a change of some other name to Peter Grant. If he had his name legally changed, he had to submit his old name, or his attorney did."

"Stone, for a lot of his life nothing was on computers, except in big cities. Your suggestion would require an enormous amount of handwork."

"Well, try the cities that have had computers for a long time. Start with Boston, where he says he's from. Also check the student records at Groton and Harvard, where he says he was educated. The rest is your problem. Good day to you, Lance." He hung up.

18

Tessa arrived at a quarter past seven, apologizing for being late.

"That's not late," Dino said, "that's fashionable."

Stone introduced everybody, then tended bar and settled everyone before the living room fireplace, which produced a brave little blaze.

"How was your day?"

"Busy," Tessa replied. "I got a request last night for a last-minute party tomorrow night, and we're all invited."

Stone looked at Dino and Viv. "Are you okay for another night in Paris?"

"We both took a week," Dino said, "which, with the weekend, is ten days."

"By Dino's count," Viv said.

"I've arranged a caterer, a musical duo, and I'm doing the staging myself."

"What sort of staging?"

"Well, our host has a good eye for art, but not for where to hang it. Same goes for small sculptures and objects. I think he's just always hung or set things down when he bought them, then forgotten about them."

"Who is our host?"

"Peter Grant."

Stone blinked. "I thought you said he was too cheap to entertain."

"I don't think I used those words, exactly," she replied. "I think *reluctant* is a better word."

"Is there an occasion?"

"I don't know. He just came up to me after dinner last night and asked if I could do it on short notice. Since short notice happens to be my métier, I said yes."

"Who else is coming?"

"I don't know; he said he'd handle the place cards."

"Do you find this event mysterious in any way?"

"What's mysterious about a dinner party?"

"Well, it's mysterious that he would invite me, on such short acquaintance. And I don't think he even met Viv and Dino last night."

"We shook his hand," Dino said.

"It was ice cold," Viv replied. "That bothers me in a man. It's downright reptilian."

"I didn't notice," Stone said.

"You would have, if he'd been a woman."

"Well, I do enjoy a cold hand on the back of the neck on a warm evening."

"I'll see what I can do," Tessa remarked. "Where are we dining? Am I correctly dressed?"

"At Tour d'Argent," Stone replied. "I had a craving for duck, which I have ordered for all of us. I hope that's all right."

"You got a table there on short notice?" Dino asked.

Stone shrugged. "Sometimes I get lucky."

Viv choked a little on her drink.

They arrived at the restaurant only a little late and were taken up in the elevator to the dining room and seated at the table with the best view in town of Notre Dame.

"I can see why you got lucky," Dino said.

Stone looked out the window at Notre Dame and found it covered in scaffolding and lit only by emergency lighting. He had forgotten about the fire. "It's hard to see it that way," he said to nobody in particular.

"Macron says he'll have it done in five years," Tessa said, "and he already has the money. Marcel gave €250,000,000, the largest donation I've heard about."

"I hope they spring for the sprinkler system this time," Dino said.

Stone had ordered for them, and they were served seared foie gras, while their duck was carved at a nearby table. They had a good claret, but not a great one, because the wine list prices were breathtaking, and Stone wasn't sure he had that much breath to spare.

Tessa leaned over when they touched glasses. "I'm glad you were able to make your companion of last evening vanish," she said.

"I had nothing to do with it. Blame the hot market for large aircraft."

"I think you're being modest."

"I have nothing to be modest about," Stone said, then thought about that for a moment. "I hope that came out right."

"So do I," Tessa said.

The duck, from the very old restaurant's own farm, was succulent and everything it was supposed to be.

Stone was talking to Tessa when she looked toward the elevator and stared. "My, look at that," she said.

"I don't think my head will turn that far," Stone said, his back to the elevator. "Who is it?"

"It's Peter Grant," she said, "with a lot of men. And he's behaving like the host. Now *that's* unusual."

"The men or him hosting?"

"Both. It's entirely out of character in a restaurant this expensive."

Stone watched the men as they passed by his table. They were slightly rough-looking, he thought, but expensively tailored and wearing, almost uniformly, loud neckties, except for Peter, who was his impeccable Charvet self.

"I heard a scrap of a foreign language as they passed us," said Dino, who was seated on the aisle.

"What language?"

"How would I know?" Dino asked. "Maybe Russian. It sounds like the way people talk in Brighton Beach, Brooklyn, which is pretty thickly Russian."

"I hope they're not coming to dinner tomorrow night," Stone said. He had had more than enough problems with Russians in his time.

"Too many," Tessa said. "Dinner tomorrow is for twelve, and there are that many at Peter's table now."

Like many large tables, they became loud as strong drink was taken. There were iced bottles of vodka on the table.

"Tessa, what do you make of Peter entertaining a crowd of Russians?"

"It can't be social," she replied. "Peter would not deign. It's got to be business."

"Do you know what business Peter is in?"

"No, he always says he invests. I pressed him on what he invests in once, and he said something about agricultural products."

"Poppies are agricultural products, of a kind," Dino said.

"My God," Stone murmured, as the sommelier approached Grant's table with a half dozen bottles on a wheeled tray and began decanting them. "He's ordered the Romanée-Conti burgundies. There's at least a hundred thousand dollars' worth of wine on that table."

"Pearls before swine," Tessa said.

S tone waited until after breakfast before phoning Lance Cabot and scrambling.

"Give me news," Lance said. "Please."

"All right, last night Peter Grant entertained a dozen Russian gentlemen, if I can apply that term to them, at Tour d'Argent, no less. I think the name translates as 'a walk around money,' or something like that."

"That sort of extravagance does not match up with reports of his parsimony," Lance said.

"I'm not finished. Grant ordered six—count 'em, *six*—bottles of the Romanée-Conti '78. I asked for the wine list later, and I reckon his bill was something like one hundred twenty thousand euros, just for the juice of the grape."

Lance was, apparently, stunned into silence.

"Not only that," Stone continued, "but also tonight he's hosting a dinner party for twelve at his home, to which we are invited."

Lance found his voice. "It would appear," he said, "that our Mr. Grant has experienced a windfall."

"Almost certainly," Stone replied. "But a windfall from what?"

"How do you know the men were Russians?" Lance asked.

"Dino caught a snatch of their conversation on the way to their table, and he said it sounded the way everybody in Brighton Beach speaks."

"How were they dressed?"

"Very good suits, but their neckties all looked as if they had been purchased at the same hot new Moscow men's shop."

"Twelve guests at Tour d'Argent at five hundred euros or so a head, plus wine, would be a lot to spend on Poles or Czechs," Lance observed. "I think Dino was right."

"Dino has a good ear."

"I need to ponder this for a while," Lance said. "Anything else?"

"Did you have any luck on the name-change search?"

"We searched Boston, Chicago, and Los Angeles," Lance said, "but came up with nothing."

"Then the next search should be of deceased men who would now be of Grant's age."

"Ah, yes, birth certificates. If we can find a Peter Grant matched up with a tombstone applying for a passport, that would be very helpful."

"I leave you with that, then," Stone said.

"Stone, I want a guest list for that dinner party tonight."

"It will be forthcoming tomorrow," Stone replied, and they both hung up.

Dino looked at him from across the breakfast table. "One hundred twenty thousand euros for wine?"

"In round numbers; I didn't want to whip out my iPhone calculator, which I normally use for simple arithmetic."

Back at Langley, Lance buzzed his secretary.

"Yes, sir?"

"Kindly google the wine list at Tour d'Argent, in Paris, and get a price per bottle for Romanée-Conti '78."

"Yes, sir." Shortly, she buzzed back.

"Do you have it?"

"Something around twenty-three thousand dollars," she replied. "I don't know what the euro is today. How many bottles would you like?"

"That will be all for the moment," Lance replied, then hung up. He wished desperately to know how Peter Grant could afford that, or if he couldn't, why he had ordered it. He called an assistant and ordered a Dun & Bradstreet report on Grant and credit checks from all three services.

An hour later, the assistant phoned back. "We drew a blank on everything," he said. "I checked the European services, too. The man doesn't seem to have so much as a credit card."

Lance called Stone and scrambled.

"Yes, Lance?"

"Did you happen to see how Mr. Grant paid his bill at Tour d'Argent last night?"

"No, we left first."

"Do you know if he has a personal chef or uses a caterer?"

"He's using a caterer tonight. An acquaintance of mine arranged it."

"Please find out by what means he pays the bill."

"I'll see what I can do." They both hung up.

As they were driving to Peter Grant's apartment, in the fashionable 8th arrondissement, Stone turned to Tessa, who was in the front passenger seat. "Would you, please, when you have the opportunity, write down the names of the guests present tonight?"

"I may not know everyone. I'll see if I can get a look at the place cards."

"Thank you."

The building was old, elegant, and in beautiful condition, as if it had recently undergone a renovation. They rode to the top floor and were admitted to a foyer, then to a large salon, which contained more gilded plaster and furniture than Stone was accustomed to, even in a French apartment. Marcel du Bois, in the company of a beautiful actress of the French cinema, was already there. Stone shook Peter's hand.

"Good evening, Stone," the man said.

"Good evening, Peter. I wonder if you could direct me to the powder room?"

"Of course," Grant replied, nodding toward a corridor leading from an interior corner of the room. "Down that hallway, second door on your left."

Stone ambled to the corridor, then hurried. He passed what must have been a coat closet on his left, then an open bedroom door on his right, then came to the powder room. The door was ajar and the light on. He walked quickly back to the bedroom, which was lit by a single lamp, and entered, looking around for a dresser or a walk-in closet. He followed a light across the room and entered a large dressing room, hung with suits and jackets arranged by color. Then he found what he was looking for: a dresser built into the room, its top scattered with the contents of Peter Grant's pockets. Stone had been correct in assuming that the host would not fill the pockets of his dinner suit with his usual belongings, since he was not going out.

There was a gold Cartier money clip, containing, no doubt, several hundred euros, as well as a black alligator wallet, containing thousands more in €1,000 and €2,000 denominations. He looked quickly through the wallet and found only a French driver's license bearing a Cap d'Antibes address—no credit cards. There was another black alligator wallet, which when opened, contained a checkbook for the Berg Bank of Zurich, an elegant private bank where Stone had once attended a business meeting. Several checks had been torn out, but the wallet contained no check register, so he could not see what payments had been made. He quickly took a jotter pad from his pocket and noted the row of digits across the bottom of the checks, then hurried from the dressing room and bedroom to the powder room. He flushed the toilet, then returned to the salon, where he rejoined Tessa, Dino, and Viv.

Stone gave Tessa his jotter and pen. "Please do your thing with the place cards."

She managed to skirt the arriving guests and move to the dining room. She returned after a few minutes and gave the pad and pen back to Stone.

He took a moment to glance through the list. There was only one Russian name: Yevgeny Chekhov, no Mrs. Chekhov. He pocketed the jotter and pen and made nice with the other guests, none of whom was Mr. Chekhov.

He noticed that Peter Grant received a brief cell phone call, then he nodded to a butler, and dinner was announced. Just as the guests were finding their places, a squarely built, middle-aged man, encased in an expensive dinner suit, arrived and was seated next to Peter. Peter rapped on his water glass with a knife. "Excuse me, ladies and gentlemen," he said. "May I introduce my good friend Yevgeny Chekhov?" Everyone nodded politely. "It is too rare that we see Yevgeny in Paris, and I am very happy that he could join us." Peter sat down, and the dinner was served.

———

The wines were a Le Montrachet 1972 with the first course and a Château Latour 1959 with the entrée, then with dessert a Château d'Yquem 1960, all on a par with Grant's largesse the evening before. The port served with the cheese course was a Quinta do Noval Nacional 1945, which Stone knew was almost impossible to obtain. He enjoyed the wines, lingering over each, and he especially loved the port.

Dino was two seats away from Chekhov, and Stone could tell his ear was cocked in that direction. Fortunately, the Russian's conversation was conducted in English. Stone noted no attempt by Peter Grant to try Russian.

After they were invited back to the salon for cognac and liqueurs, Stone managed to edge over to the Russian and engage him in conversation. "Where have you come to us from, Mr. Chekhov?" he asked.

Chekhov looked at him as if he were mad or an imbecile. "From St. Petersburg," he replied. "I was there this morning." He spoke English with a faintly British accent.

"Ah, a lovely city," Stone said, though he had never been there.

"On behalf of the Russian people, I thank you for your compliment," Chekhov replied.

"In what capacity do you speak for the Russian people?" Stone asked, smiling.

"Huh?" Chekhov blurted out.

"I thought, perhaps, you were the Russian ambassador to France."

"Why would you think that?" the man asked.

"Because you spoke on behalf of the Russian people," Stone replied, keeping his smile fixed.

"I have no idea what you are talking about," Chekhov said, then turned on his heel and walked to where Peter Grant stood, apparently reporting his conversation with the American fool.

Dino came over. "Enjoy your chat with Chekhov?"

"Yes," Stone replied, "but he apparently did not." He related what had been said.

"It was something like that when I tried to engage him over dinner. He seemed to want to speak only to Grant, even ignored the beautiful woman between us."

"Could you hear what he and Grant were talking about?"

"Agricultural products," Dino said, "at least for a moment."

"Which ones?"

"I had the impression that that part of the conversation was entirely for my benefit," Dino said, "and it was very thin."

"Did you enjoy the wines?"

"My God, yes," Dino replied. "I'm pretty drunk."

"So am I," Stone said. "Why don't you fake a heart attack so we can get out of here?"

"Ladies and gentlemen!" Peter Grant nearly shouted. "My friend Mr. Chekhov regrets that he must leave us, and he has asked me to wish you all a good evening."

Chekhov managed a grimace, then with a backward wave of his hand, pontiff style, he marched out of the apartment, followed by a large man in a business suit with a bulge in his left armpit.

Since the apparent guest of honor had departed, the others be-gan to drift out, and soon Stone and his party were back in the old Mercedes convertible.

"Those were the most spectacular wines I've ever drunk," Tessa said, and there were murmurs of agreement from the others.

"Tessa," Stone said, "I think Peter spent something like a hun-dred twenty thousand euros on wine last evening, and probably considerably more tonight. You spoke of him as tight with his money. Can you account for his sudden largesse the past two evenings?"

"I cannot," Tessa said, "unless he's broken the bank at Monte Carlo, and we're a long way from Monte Carlo."

"Have you ever known him to splurge before?"

"Never at any time," she replied. "I've bought more drinks for him than he has for me. Until tonight."

"Do you know how he paid his caterer tonight?"

"No, I imagine he's probably taking care of that about now."

"Have you ever known him to use a credit card?"

She thought about it. "No, on those occasions when he does pay, he seems always to use cash."

"In euros?"

"I think so."

"Have you ever been gambling with him?"

"No. Sorry, yes. Once, in Monte Carlo. He was very cautious, and he managed to win a bit, though not enough to buy those wines. Why are you so interested in his spending habits?"

"Because his behavior is so at odds with what I've been told about him, mostly by you."

"Well, the horses are running at Longchamp," she said. "Perhaps somebody gave him a tip, or a long shot came in."

"Do you have any idea who that fellow, Chekhov, is?"

"No, but he was at Tour d'Argent with Peter's group last night, sitting next to Peter."

"Have you seen Peter in the company of Russians before?"

"No. Last night and tonight are the only times I've seen Peter in company that he assembled himself. All the other parties or dinners were given by others, with their guests." She turned her body on the car seat to face him. "Tell me, Stone, what is your interest in Peter? We never seem to talk about anything else."

"I apologize," Stone said. "Why don't we talk about something else?"

"I have a question," she said, as they pulled into his garage and everyone got out of the car.

"Please ask it."

"Why haven't you made the slightest pass at me since we met? It's all right if you're gay, Stone, just tell me."

Stone took her upstairs and demonstrated that he was not.

Early the following morning, Stone was awakened by a nuzzle from Tessa, which quickly evolved into a fondle. He responded as a gentleman should, and soon they were entwined.

"May we have breakfast in bed?" Tessa asked as soon as they had both caught their breath.

"We may," Stone replied, and called Marie on the house phone with the request, leaving the menu to her. Another forty minutes of nuzzling and fondling ensued, then there was a ringing noise. "Dumbwaiter," he said.

He got out of bed, then carried two trays over and set them down on the bedcover. One tray contained dishes, utensils, and the *Times*, the other contained a single platter adorned with softly scrambled eggs, back bacon, fat Normandy sausages, and small pancakes. A pitcher of syrup stood beside the platter, along with another of orange juice and a silver pot of coffee.

"Let me serve," Tessa said. Stone got back into bed and watched her build his breakfast. Finally, she returned with her own.

"I'm sorry about what I said last night," she said. "I didn't really think you were gay."

"Quite all right. I had been neglecting you and, given your charms, that was inexcusable."

"You've more than made up for any neglect," she said, then plunged into her breakfast.

When they had finished, they could only lie there and sip coffee from cups resting on their bellies. Stone's cell phone rang, and he held a finger to his lips. Tessa nodded, then closed her eyes.

"Yes, Lance?" Stone said.

"Scramble."

"Scrambled."

"Read me the guest list from last night," Lance said.

Stone picked up his jotter from the bedside table and read the list, saving Chekhov for last.

"What was that last name?" Lance asked.

"Yevgeny Chekhov, like the playwright."

Lance sucked in a breath. "I don't believe it," he said.

"Well, I didn't pat him down for an ID, I just took Peter's word for it. Oh, he was at the Tour d'Argent dinner the night before, too."

"Do you have any idea who you're talking about?" Lance asked.

"Ah, middle-aged, strongly built, balding."

"I mean: Do you know who he is?"

"I haven't the foggiest," Stone replied.

"I expect you are aware that after Kronsky was elected as Russia's president, he assembled a group of his friends and doled out to them control of previously government-owned industries, at bargain prices. Those men are known, collectively, as the oligarchy."

"I believe I've seen that information in the *Times* on a few hundred occasions."

"Well, Chekhov is the closest to Kronsky and, thus, the richest and most powerful among them. We estimate his wealth, spread around the world, to be about *a hundred and eighty billion dollars.*"

"Gulp," Stone said. "Did I get the number of zeros right?"

"You did. What is more, this is the first occasion, of which I am aware, that he has been seen outside of Russia, and I tend to keep track of such things. He is also very strongly connected with Russian intelligence. He and Kronsky were classmates at the KGB University."

"All right, I'm impressed. What do you suppose brings him to Paris?"

"How should I know? That's what I want *you* to find out!"

"Lance," Stone said. "I spoke with Mr. Chekhov briefly last evening, and he exhibits a rather regal mien. He does not suffer fools gladly, and he has clearly assigned me to membership in that group."

"What on earth did you say to him?"

Stone took Lance through their conversation. "He seemed to think he spoke for the Russian people in all things. I'm afraid that amused me."

"You *laughed* at Yevgeny Chekhov?"

"I'd like to think I laughed *with* him. But it's entirely possible, in fact probable, that he did not see it that way."

"And I thought I could count on you to be discreet," Lance groaned.

"I had no instructions regarding discretion, or on how to kowtow to a Russian oligarch," Stone said. "So I treated him like a normal human being."

"He is *not* a normal human being," Lance said, "as I assume you now understand."

"I understand that he does not regard *himself* as a normal human being," Stone said, "and that he may have come to regard me as less than one, since he is obviously accustomed to a level of obsequiousness that I have not yet attained in my dealings with the superrich."

"Oh, stop being such a pompous ass," Lance scolded.

"I believe that, on this occasion, Mr. Chekhov more resembled the referenced creature."

"He's entitled to behave like an ass: he has a hundred and eighty billion dollars! Do you realize that makes him the second richest person on earth, after President Kronsky himself, whom we believe to have two hundred and twenty billion?"

"In my passing experience with a handful of persons of very lofty wealth, I have found them, for the most part, to be kind, charming, and endearingly modest about their station in life."

"Were any of them Russian?"

"Well, no, but . . ."

"Endearing modesty is not a detectable trait of Russians who have accumulated great wealth through nefarious means," Lance said. "If you insist on that sort of behavior from them, you will soon find yourself reposing in a barrel of fish in the Black Sea."

"All the more reason for me to never again clap eyes on Yevgeny Chekhov," Stone replied firmly. "Now, if you'll excuse me, my breakfast is getting cold." He hung up.

Tessa was staring at him. "Was that Lance Cabot on the phone?"

"How did you know that?" Stone asked.

"It came to me in a flash when you called him 'Lance.'"

"I don't believe I called him that."

"I believe you did. Do you know who Lance Cabot is?"

"Of course I know who he is. Why else would I be on a transatlantic call with him?"

"You were talking on the phone with Lance Cabot about Yevgeny Chekhov?"

"We were discussing his relation to the playwright, Anton Chekhov," Stone replied. "I believe they are fourth cousins, twice removed. Lance disagrees."

"How do you know Lance Cabot?" she asked.

"How do *you* know him?"

"I don't, but I read the *New York Times*'s international edition every day," she said, grabbing the newspaper from the breakfast tray. "You don't mind if I do the crossword, do you?"

"Help yourself," said Stone, who minded a very great deal.

Tessa did the *Times* crossword faster than Stone felt she had any right to, then she set the paper on his belly. "All yours," she said. "Now, come on, tell me how you know Lance Cabot."

Stone reached over to the bedside table, found his small pocket wallet, extracted a card from it, and silently handed it to her.

Tessa gazed at it, then her eyes widened. "'Special Adviser to the Director?'" she read. "You're a spy?"

Stone took some satisfaction from her wonder, since he had not yet given one of his new cards to anyone. "I am not a spy," he said. "On occasion, I am asked by the director for advice on one thing or another."

"You're a spy," she said, pointing at the card. "It says so right there."

"Read it again. It does not say I'm a spy, quite the contrary."

"But that's what it *means*, doesn't it?"

"It does not. It means what it says. Please don't misinterpret."

"I've never met a spy before."

"Of course you have. What do you think Peter Grant is?"

"Peter? That's the most ridiculous thing I've ever heard."

"Why do you say that?"

"He doesn't have the brains for it, that's why."

"Do you know who Yevgeny Chekhov is?"

"Well, not until last night."

"Who is he?"

"A Russian? Christ, I don't know."

"He was a classmate of President Kronsky at the KGB University, when they were very young. He maintains very close ties with Russian intelligence. Oh, and he happens to be the second richest man in the world, after Kronsky. He has a net worth of one hundred eighty billion dollars."

"Now, *that's* impressive! I don't suppose he needs a date tonight?"

"If he does, Peter will arrange it. But if he invites you, turn him down—in the most courteous possible way."

"So why does this make Peter a spy?" she asked.

"Two reasons: One, why else would Chekhov be hanging out with him? Two, where is Peter getting his newfound wealth?"

"I don't know, and I don't know."

The bedside house phone rang, and Stone picked it up. "Yes, Marie?"

"A Mr. Rick to see you down here."

"Thank you, Marie. Give him a cup of coffee and tell him I'll be down in twenty minutes." He hung up. "Will you excuse me, Tessa? I have a visitor downstairs."

"Who is he?"

"A spy." Stone headed for the shower.

When Stone came downstairs, Rick La Rose seemed to be dozing in his chair. "Good morning, Rick," he said loudly.

Rick opened his eyes. "Good morning, Stone. Forgive my state. I had a long night."

"Would you like a second cup of coffee?"

"Please."

Stone rang for Marie and placed the order. "Now," he said, "to what do I owe the pleasure?"

"I heard a rumor that Yevgeny Chekhov is in Paris."

"I expect you heard that from Lance. It's quite true. What do you know about Chekhov?"

"Just what's in his file. I'm sure you've been told that."

"Have you no personal information about him?"

Rick shrugged. "He likes his women two at a time, and he's nuts about French wines. That's about it."

"I can confirm the part about the wines," Stone said. "For the past two nights I've watched him drink them."

"Where?"

"At Tour d'Argent and at Peter Grant's apartment. Grant was his host on both occasions." He recited the wines served at both dinners.

"Holy shit," Rick said.

"Me, too. Lance wants to know where Grant got the money. My bet is from Chekhov."

"You won't lose money on that bet," Rick replied.

"Lance wants to know everything about Chekhov," Stone said. "That's a job for you, not me."

"Thanks for your help," Rick said drily.

"I don't have any sources for that sort of information," Stone said. "I wouldn't know where to start."

"Well, you're possibly the only person in the Western Hemisphere who's had a conversation with him," Rick pointed out. "Not counting Peter Grant."

"It was a very brief and unproductive conversation," Stone replied. The phone on the table beside him rang. "Yes? Good morning." He listened for a moment. "Why me?" Long pause. "All right." He hung up.

"Anything I should know about?" Rick asked.

"That was Peter Grant. Yevgeny Chekhov has invited me to have lunch with him today, in the garden of the Russian embassy."

"I thought he didn't like you."

"Maybe he wants to poison me," Stone said.

S tone dressed in a blue suit and a sober necktie, googled the
address of the Russian embassy, and drove himself there. He
looked for a parking space and didn't find one, so he parked
directly in front of the building, practically in the face of an armed,
uniformed guard, who spoke to him harshly in French.

"English?" Stone asked.

"Da. Yes."

"My name is Barrington. I have a luncheon appointment with
Yevgeny Chekhov."

The soldier blinked.

"Please mind my car," Stone said, getting out. The soldier
opened the gate for him. "The keys are in it," Stone said, walking
to the front door, which opened a second before he arrived.

A man in a black suit stood there. "Mr. Barrington?" he asked.

"I am."

"Will you follow me, please?" He led Stone past the grand stair-
case in the lobby to a hallway behind it, then to double doors at the
end, which opened for them.

"Please," his escort said, motioning him to a seating area at one end of a large office. "Mr. Chekhov will be with you momentarily."

Stone took a seat and waited. A stack of Russian newspapers was placed on the coffee table before him, and he picked up one.

"Do you read Russian?" a voice behind him asked.

Stone turned to see a door behind him and Yevgeny Chekhov entering, followed by Peter Grant.

"No," Stone said. "I was just looking at the pictures."

"Good afternoon," Chekhov said, offering his hand.

"Good afternoon," Stone replied, rising and shaking it. "So you are, after all, the ambassador from the Russian Federation?"

"No," Chekhov replied, "the ambassador is temporarily in Moscow, for consultations. I am merely borrowing his office and, more important, his garden, where we shall have luncheon." His accent was still slightly British, and he wore what passed for a small smile.

Peter said nothing, but offered his hand.

"Come this way, please," Chekhov said, then led them past the ambassador's desk and through French doors behind it into an enclosed garden, nicely planted, where a table for three had been set. They sat down, and immediately two waiters appeared and served them with bowls of borscht.

"My native cuisine," Chekhov said. "I hope you don't mind."

"I'm very fond of borscht," Stone said. A waiter added a dollop of sour cream to it, and Stone took a sip. "Excellent," he said.

"I wish to apologize for being abrupt with you last evening," Chekhov said. "I plead jet lag."

"Not at all," Stone said, enjoying his soup. Peter Grant said nothing, just ate.

"By the way, Peter," Stone said, "I wanted to tell you how much

I enjoyed dinner last night, particularly the wines, which were spectacular."

"Thank you," Peter replied. "The wines were chosen by Mr. Chekhov, from his own cellar."

"That is a cellar I would like to visit sometime," Stone said.

"Then we will arrange that," Chekhov said, "on your next visit to Moscow."

"That would be my first visit to Moscow," Stone said, "and I would like a visit to your cellar very much."

"Do you collect wines, Mr. Barrington?" Chekhov asked.

"In a small way—enough for my occasional dinner guests. Marcel du Bois, whom you met last evening, is kind enough to send me a case or two now and then."

"Ah, Mr. du Bois," Chekhov said. "I'm told he is the richest man in Europe."

Stone shrugged. "Moscow is in Europe, is it not?"

Chekhov actually managed a laugh. "I presume you are referring to our president."

"Of course."

"Perhaps he may be. I have not seen his financial statement."

"Has he seen yours?" Stone couldn't resist asking.

"Mr. Kronsky knows all," Chekhov said.

"I find it unusual that both you and he have names from Russian literature."

"We Russians love our literature," Chekhov replied. "My name at birth has too many syllables to be comfortable for Westerners and, indeed, for many Russians. I chose a new one when I entered university."

"What university did you attend?" Stone asked.

Chekhov hesitated before answering. "A military one," he replied finally.

"Is it true that you and Mr. Kronsky were classmates there?"

Chekhov looked at him sharply. "You are the first person ever to ask me that," he said.

"Am I?" Stone asked.

"You are, and the answer is yes. The president and I first became acquainted there—actually, on the day we took our entrance examinations. We were numbers one and two in the rankings of the examinees."

Stone wanted to ask who was number one, but he resisted.

"Kronsky was first," Chekhov said.

"What was your major course of study there?" Stone asked.

"Western languages," Chekhov replied, "and economics, a subject that has always interested me. And you? Where did you study?"

"At New York University, which was a few blocks from my home. Both undergraduate and law school."

"Ah, the law. That has always interested me, too, but in the Soviet Union of my day, the law was rather a fluid subject. Or, at least, fluidly applied."

"After law school I was a policeman for some years," Stone said. "Perhaps we share that?"

"Yes, I was a policeman, too, but . . . How shall I put it? A political policeman."

Stone didn't need that explained.

Their soup bowls were replaced with plates of chicken breasts, which a waiter took a knife to, and garlic butter flowed. Chicken Kiev.

Stone tasted his. "Delicious."

"I understand that you also have an interest in economics," Chekhov said. "Or rather, perhaps, in investment."

"I do. I belong to a partnership that invests for both my son's trust fund and for me."

"I trust you both profited handsomely from the recent IPO."

That stopped Stone in his tracks. How could Chekhov know about that?

"Peter and I did rather well with it," Chekhov said, with another of his almost-smiles.

The subject then changed quickly to racehorses, where Stone was out of his depth, then to American movies.

"My son is a movie director," Stone said, "and I serve on the board of Centurion Studios."

"Centurion!" Chekhov erupted. "They have a distinguished catalog! I have seen it all in my time. What is your son's name?"

"Peter Barrington."

"Aha! I have seen two of his. Excellent! He will have a long and successful career."

"I'll tell him you said so."

They were served ice cream, then moved to some outdoor furniture for coffee.

"Tell me," Chekhov said. "Any tips?"

"Movie tips?" Stone asked.

Chekhov's eyes narrowed. "Investment tips," he said.

"I'm afraid that, as a partner in my investment firm, I am unable to discuss that with you under penalty of a law called insider trading."

"I am familiar with the term," Chekhov said, "but it seems to me something that should not stand between friends."

So they were now friends? "Even if I were inclined to break the law—for friends—I am held somewhat at arm's length by my investing partner, who is a stickler for following the law."

Chekov's smile disappeared, and his eyes grew cold. "I am disappointed to hear that," he said. "It smacks of distrust between friends."

"I hope we will become friends, in spite of that," Stone said, glancing at his watch. "If you will kindly excuse me, I have another appointment. I thank you so much for the delicious lunch and the agreeable company."

He shook both their hands and turned toward the main building, where the previous attendant led him from the building.

His car was parked where he had left it, and the guard handed him his keys. Stone extended his hand to be shaken, startling the guard. "I thank you for your kind attention to my car."

The guard shifted his automatic weapon to his left hand and extended his right. Stone shook it, pressing a fifty-euro note into the man's palm, which he did not reject.

Stone drove away, enjoying the Paris afternoon in the open car.

S tone's cell phone was ringing as he walked into the house.

"Yes, Lance?"

"Scramble."

"Scrambled."

"Tell me all," Lance said.

"About what?" Stone asked innocently.

"Did I explain that I have the facility of sending a powerful electric shock to your new iPhone?"

"You mean about Yevgeny Chekhov?"

"However did you guess?"

"We had a very pleasant lunch in the ambassador's private garden, that gentleman being in Moscow for consultations. We had borscht, then Chicken Kiev, then ice cream."

Lance remained silent, waiting.

Stone told him all.

"You mean, all he wanted was stock tips?"

"That was all. He said that both he and Peter had done well on our latest IPO, which explains Peter's recent largesse—except for the wines, which I was told came from Chekhov's own cellar."

"Last night's, not those at Tour d'Argent."

"Quite right, Peter would have had to pay for those, but then he did very well with the IPO."

"How did you react to Chekhov's request for stock tips?"

"I explained to him the law against insider trading," Stone replied.

"How did he take that?"

"He called me his friend, and tried again."

"I hope you gave him something?"

"I did not," Stone replied. "First of all, I don't have any tips at my disposal, but even if I had, I wouldn't have given them to him. In fact, I thought of reporting him to the Securities and Exchange Commission."

"Stone, if you had done that and they had subsequently suspended him from trading on American markets . . ."

"I know, I'd be in a barrel of fish in the Black Sea."

"Quite. But perhaps, if we are patient, we will have another opportunity to report him, one that cannot be traced to you. I would love to see the son of a bitch suspended from trading in the U.S."

"So would I, and Peter Grant, too, for abetting him."

"At least we now know where Grant's funds come from."

"Did I tell you what I did at Peter's apartment?"

"Just the wines."

"I also feigned a need for the toilet and sneaked into my host's dressing room."

"What did you find there? Dresses?"

"A lot of Charvet and Huntsman suits, but also his wallet and his checkbook."

"Tell me about the checkbook."

"It had no register, so I could not see what checks he had written, but his account is with the Berg Bank of Zurich, and several checks had been torn out."

"Do you know the Berg Bank?"

"I dealt with them briefly on behalf of the estate of Eduardo Bianchi, which had a large sum on deposit there that I wanted back."

"Were you able to retrieve it?"

"Yes, though they were unhappy about it."

"That sounds like them. It's often said of the bank that they would be happy to open a deposit account for Satan himself."

Stone laughed. "I can believe that. Would you like Peter's account number?"

"Yes, please, I might be able to do something with that."

Stone read it from his jotter.

"Thank you. I expect that Peter must have a debit card on that account, which would explain why he never uses credit cards."

"I wonder what his balance is?"

"Perhaps you could find out," Lance suggested. "Call your friend Charley Fox, and see what he can learn about what Peter made on the IPO."

"I'll try that," Stone said.

"In the meantime, I may have a source at Berg."

"I wouldn't be surprised," Stone replied.

"Anything else to report?"

"Nothing," Stone said. They both hung up, and Stone called Charley Fox.

"Yeah?"

"It's Stone. I hope I'm not disturbing you."

"You're not disturbing anything. What can I do you for?"

"I wonder if you can find out what participation in our recent IPO two men had."

"Their names?"

"Yevgeny Chekhov, a Russian oligarch, and Peter Grant, an American living in France."

"Never heard of the first guy, but I know Peter Grant."

"How?" Stone asked.

"I met him at a dinner party a year, maybe eighteen months ago."

"Funny, he says he hasn't been back to the States for decades. Where did you meet him?"

"At the home of some friends in New York."

"Was that the first time you met him?"

"And the last, so far. I'd had a couple of drinks, and I may have said more than I should've about the IPO, even though it was way ahead of the event."

"That explains how Peter found out, and he probably reported back to Chekhov. Can you find out what they had invested and how much they sold?"

"Maybe. I'll check the records of the sales later and get back to you."

"Excellent. I'd appreciate it if you could discreetly ask around about Chekhov. I'm inclined to think he's probably broken a law or two. But be careful. We don't want word reaching him that you've been asking questions about him."

"Then I'll see what I can learn on the computer," Charley said. "Talk to you tomorrow."

"Thank you, Charley." Stone hung up.

———

Later in the afternoon Dino and Viv came downstairs from a nap, and Stone made them a drink. They had just begun drinking it when Tessa Martindale came in, bearing shopping bags. "I want one of those," she said, "whatever they are."

Stone poured her a vodka gimlet, and she sat down.

"What have you done with your day?" Stone asked.

"Lunched with a friend and gossiped."

"About whom?"

"Peter Grant."

"What did you learn?"

"That Peter was seen writing a large check at Charvet," she said. "Apparently, his account had fallen into arrears."

"How large a check?"

"My friend got a glimpse of it while she was waiting. It was for twenty-something thousand euros."

"Whew!" Dino said. "I hope I never get a tailor's bill for that much."

"Not much chance of that," Viv said, elbowing him.

"What? You'd like me to spend more?"

"Yes, I would. You've lost some weight, and that's a perfect excuse."

"Stone, do I have time to order a suit at Charvet?"

"Yes, but not to get a first fitting. You'll have to wait for your next trip to Paris for that."

"Gives us an excuse to come back," Viv said.

They dined on Marie's cooking and stayed up late talking. Later, Tessa was insistent in bed, then woke Stone up again in the middle of the night. As a result, he overslept.

He was awakened by the ringing of his cell phone on the bedside table. "Hello," he muttered.

"Is it early there?" Charley Fox asked.

Stone glanced at the bedside clock. "No, it's nearly noon. Did you find anything?"

"Well, as you can imagine, a lot of investors jumped in at the first opportunity, but the names you gave me didn't appear. I tried various ways of limiting my search criteria, and I came up with one very interesting transaction. A Swiss corporation, called Acme Ltd., had apparently acquired a large block of stock from the previous owner, St. Clair, from whose estate we bought control. Acme sold all day, in chunks, then continued to sell on other markets. The total income from all those transactions was three hundred and sixty-two million dollars. I haven't been able to find out who owns Acme, but it sounds like your friend Chekhov. Peter Grant doesn't come into it."

"Perhaps Chekhov gave Grant a cut for services rendered."

"Could be. I remembered something else about Peter Grant: he knew James St. Clair, whose name came up in conversation."

"How well?"

"He made out that they were intimates. Perhaps he bought stock from St. Clair in anticipation of an IPO."

"I don't think he would have the capital for that kind of transaction, but his friend Chekhov could certainly write that check."

"Acme teamed up with the Berg Bank of Zurich to make its sales. That would help calm suspicions that Acme was doing all the dumping."

"And Peter Grant has an account at the Berg Bank."

"I believe the word is: Aha!"

"That could very well be the word," Stone said. "Thanks, Charley, you done good."

"My pleasure." Charley hung up.

Stone called Lance and told him what Charley Fox had just told him.

"That gives me something to check with my source at Berg. Bye." Lance hung up.

Tessa came out of the bathroom with a towel wrapped around her, but she discarded it and jumped into bed. "I hope you like making love to clean women," she said.

"You have sapped all my precious bodily fluids," Stone said. "I think you need at least two other lovers to keep you occupied."

"Is that an invitation to a foursome?" she asked hopefully.

"God help me, no. It is a plea for rest and recuperation," Stone whimpered.

"You're no fun at all," she pouted.

"Wasn't that fun last night? All two times?"

"That was last night," she said, "this is today."

"The demands of your body are greater than my body can meet, in the time allotted. We've got one more night in Paris. Can you hold it in until then?"

"I'll try," Tessa said, "but I'm not promising."

"I trust the shower is free now," Stone said, struggling out of bed. "Please don't join me." He locked the bathroom door behind him.

Stone shaved, showered, and dressed, then went downstairs.

Dino put down his *Times*. "You look . . . ah . . ."

"Haggard?" Stone offered.

"That's the word."

"It's a good thing we're leaving tomorrow," Stone said. "If Tessa tries to get aboard the airplane, shoot her."

"It's as bad as that, is it?"

"It's as good as that," Stone said, "but too much of a good thing."

"I'm trying to understand," Dino said, "and failing."

"You are an unsympathetic person," Stone replied. "Lunch?"

"Why not?"

Stone sent Marie out for lobsters, and she put together a perfect lobster salad. They washed it down with a Chassagne-Montrachet Stone found in the fridge, after which the women excused themselves for one last assault on Paris retail.

Stone got a call at mid-afternoon. "Hello?"

"Scramble."

"Scrambled. What's up?" Stone asked.

"My source at the Berg Bank came up with some enlightening information: Acme is Chekhov and the balances in the account correspond to the sales in your IPO."

"That's not a surprise," Stone said.

"What's surprising is that Acme transferred twenty-five million dollars to Peter Grant's account."

"That's very generous for inside information," Stone said, "but somehow, I think Chekhov is too greedy to throw money around like that."

"Well, he's been throwing it around for the past two years, if Grant's balances are correct. The question that arises is: What does Grant have to sell that is so valuable to a Russian oligarch?"

"How are you going to find the answer to that question?" Stone asked.

"Any suggestions?"

"Kidnap Peter Grant and torture the information out of him."

"Sadly, we can't do that anymore," Lance said. "Any other suggestions?"

"Find out from somebody else besides me," Stone said. "I am drained of information about Peter Grant."

"Well," Lance said, "you're going to have one more shot at him. Make the most of it." He hung up, leaving Stone staring at his phone, wondering what the hell he was talking about.

Tessa and Viv showed up at the cocktail hour and settled themselves in Stone's living room, while he poured the gimlets.

"Oh," Tessa said, "I almost forgot. We ran into Peter Grant at

Fouquet this afternoon, when we stopped in for coffee. When I mentioned that you were all leaving for New York tomorrow morning, he asked if he could hitch a ride."

One more shot, indeed, Stone thought. "Sure. Tell him to be at Landmark Aviation, Le Bourget, tomorrow morning at nine sharp."

He called Captain Jim and gave him the news about their departure time and the added passenger.

26

Stone spent much of his night keeping his promise to Tessa, then, oddly enough, woke up feeling rested and refreshed, while Tessa was groggy. Perhaps there was some justice in the world, he mused.

A hired car drove them all to Le Bourget, including Tessa, who had a good look at the airplane, and then took the car back to Paris.

Stone and the Bacchettis had settled themselves aboard by nine AM, but there was no sign of Peter Grant. Captain Jim came aboard. "I believe you have a fourth passenger coming? Immigration is here, and they want to see his passport."

Stone glanced at his watch.

"We're ready to tow out of the hangar," Jim said.

"Give our missing passenger till the tower time, and ask Immigration to wait. Then, when you're ready, let's button up, start up, and taxi," Stone said. "He can buy himself an airline ticket."

Jim gave him a little salute. "Yes, sir." He went about his work.

Soon he came up the airstairs into the cabin. "Ready to start engines?" he asked Stone.

Stone gave him the twirling finger gesture, and Jim closed and locked the door, then went into the cockpit. A tug towed the G-500 out of its hangar, turned it ninety degrees to its right to avoid the backwash striking the hangar, then the right engine spun up and started.

Dino, who was in a window seat on the left side of the airplane, said, "Hey, there's a car at our wingtip, and somebody's getting out."

"Is it Peter Grant?"

"Yes, and the Immigration car is pulling up, too."

Stone picked up a phone and pressed the intercom button. "Jim, looks like our passenger has arrived."

"I see him. Shall we leave him in the dust?"

"No, let's get him aboard."

Julie came back to the main cabin and opened the airstairs door, which lowered itself into place. Peter Grant came aboard carrying a briefcase, followed by a uniformed chauffeur struggling with a lot of luggage. Fortunately, there was interior access to the rear luggage compartment. After letting the driver out, Julie closed and locked the door once again, then headed forward.

Peter, breathing hard, sat himself down in a seat opposite Stone. "Were you leaving without me?"

Stone glanced at his watch. "You're twenty minutes late. If you'd been one minute later, you could have watched us take off."

"Sorry, I didn't know it was time-critical."

"I believe Tessa told you nine AM *sharp*."

"Right, won't happen again."

The left engine spun up and started, and Julie came over to where Peter was sitting. "Good morning, Mr. Grant. Would you like breakfast? We'll be serving in about fifteen minutes, as soon as we're at altitude."

"Yes, thank you."

She gave him a dazzling smile and went forward to take her seat.

"Fasten your seat belt," Stone said to Peter.

Peter stood up, shed his jacket, sat back down, and strapped in. They began to taxi, and Julie came back, took his jacket, and hung it in the forward closet. Two minutes later they swung onto runway twenty-seven and, without slowing, came up to takeoff speed and rotated. The airplane's huge windows gave them good views of Paris to the south.

"This is a *very* nice airplane," Peter said. "Chekhov has a Gulfstream, but yours is more handsomely decorated."

"Thank you," Stone said, reaching into his jacket's breast pocket and switching on a small recorder concealed in his silk pocket square. "Tell me, Peter Grant, how, exactly, did you meet Yevgeny Chekhov?"

"We were introduced by a mutual friend, in Moscow."

"And who was that?"

"Dmitri Kronsky—before he became president."

"Really? How did you come to know Kronsky?"

"I had met him some years before he became president, at a party at the American ambassador's residence."

"How was Kronsky occupying himself in the days before he achieved high office?"

"He was head of the KGB, as it then was."

"How were you occupying yourself at that time?"

"I was facilitating relations between the Americans and the Russians," Peter replied.

"You must need to know a lot of Russians before you can facilitate," Stone said. "How does an American get access to those circles in Moscow?"

"Through every possible means: contacts, referrals from others, and a great deal of applied charm."

"Does charm work with Russians?"

"It works with practically everybody: witness your approach to Yevgeny Chekhov."

"I didn't approach him," Stone said, "and I didn't invite him to lunch."

"I believe he apologized for his brusqueness at your first meeting, at my home. He didn't know who you were at that point."

"But now he knows who I am?"

"I briefed him at the first opportunity. He was late arriving, if you recall."

"Would you be kind enough to repeat that briefing for my benefit? I'd like to know who Chekhov thinks I am."

Peter gave a little shrug. "You are a native New Yorker, educated in the city, who served as a police detective for many years before using your law degree to join a prominent New York law firm, of which you later became a partner. You have become widely known in the city. You are also a personal adviser to the director of the Central Intelligence Agency, with a titular rank of deputy director, and are close friends with your president, your former president, and the secretary of state. I guess that about sums you up."

"You neglected to mention my relationship with Triangle Investments, which conducted the IPO in which Mr. Chekhov and you did so well."

"Ah, that's right, Chekhov told you we profited from that," Peter said.

"He, to the tune of three hundred and sixty million dollars. You, somewhat less. How long have you been profiting from your relationship with Chekhov?"

"Long enough to keep me quite comfortable," Peter replied. "And remember, he is not the only client I advise."

"But he is the only client who could come up with a twenty-five-million-dollar contribution to your well-being, is he not?"

Peter's face fell. "Certainly not."

"And yet, until very recently you were quite deeply in debt to establishments like Charvet, where your account was in serious arrears."

"I have no debts," Peter said, huffily.

"Well, not anymore," Stone said. "Not since Chekhov wrote you that check."

"You are very well informed," Peter said, recovering his good nature.

"And I hope soon to be even better informed," Stone said. "After all, it's a seven-hour flight."

Julie appeared with breakfast trays, interrupting their conversation.

They had their breakfast and coffee pretty much in silence, high over the Atlantic. As Julie took away their trays and coffee cups, Stone said to her, "Please bring Mr. Grant another cup of coffee. We don't want him dozing off when there's so much to talk about."

Dino, as if on cue, unbuckled his seat belt and moved across the aisle, next to Peter, then rebuckled.

"What is this?" Peter asked, looking at Dino, then back at Stone.

"It's get-acquainted time," Stone said. "Where were you born, Peter?"

"In Cambridge, Massachusetts, fifty-nine years ago."

"At what hospital?"

"At home. There was a miscalculation."

"Who and what were your parents?"

"My father was a stockbroker with what was then Merrill Lynch, Pierce, Fenner & Beane, and my mother was a painter."

"Pictures or houses?"

"Pictures. She was very good."

"So was my mother."

"Matilda Stone?"

"You have the advantage of me. What are your parents' names?"

"Richard and Marion, maiden name Wright, both deceased."

"And where were you schooled?"

"Groton and Harvard."

"Your major at Harvard?"

"Journalism."

"And did you work on the *Crimson*?"

"Yes, I was assistant editor."

"How about the *Lampoon*?"

"No, I wasn't funny enough."

"What was your first job out of Harvard?"

"Copy boy at the *Boston Globe*."

"What sort of career did you have in journalism?"

"A brief one," Peter replied. "I became a reporter on the city desk, and then I met someone who convinced me that my talents were being wasted."

"Who was that?"

"A girl, one who knew a lot of people I didn't know."

"Name?"

"Ashley Dunham."

Stone's eyes narrowed. "Any relation to Howard Dunham?" The man had been a State Department official and had been accused of communist ties. Shortly after that, he had left the country and had lived in France for many years.

"She was his granddaughter," Peter said.

"Did she introduce you to him?"

"Yes, we went to Paris together. She went home after the summer, and I stayed."

"Mr. Dunham must have introduced you to a lot of interesting people."

"He did. Howard knew everybody, and he was frequently visited by American left-wing intellectuals."

"And Russians?"

"Naturally, he had contacts there."

"Did he visit Russia often?"

"Yes, he was a lover of theater and dance. When the Bolshoi came to Paris, he always hosted a big party for the company. It's a little-known fact that he was instrumental in the defection of the dancer Rudolf Nureyev."

"How so?"

"He arranged to get him away from the company minders at the airport, where he turned himself in to the police and asked for asylum. Howard supported him in many ways after that."

"Did he support you?"

"He was kind enough to help now and then. He introduced me to George Plimpton, who gave me a job at the *Paris Review*, not that it paid very much."

"Then?"

"A friend got me a job with the *Guide Michelin*, and I traveled France, rating restaurants and gaining weight steadily. I finally had to quit because I couldn't afford the alterations to my wardrobe, such as it was."

"When did you first travel to Russia?" Stone asked.

Peter looked out the window and seemed to be deciding whether to answer. Finally, he did. "Almost thirty years ago. Howard bought me a ticket on an Intourist tour and gave me a letter to a friend of his, Georgi Arbatov, who was head of the Institute of

U.S. and Canadian Studies, or ISKRAN, at the Russian Academy of Sciences. I left my tour and stayed in the country for several weeks. Arbatov knew absolutely everyone in the government and academia, and he made many introductions for me."

"Anyone among them KGB?"

"One never knew," Peter said, "though one could suspect."

"And whom did you suspect?"

"Everyone. When in Leningrad, I actually met a young officer named Vladimir Putin. Of course, I had no idea of what his future would be."

"What did you think of him?"

"He could be charming, in a cold sort of way. I had the impression he was a comer, and I wondered what happened to him after Gorbachev came into power."

"Yes, whatever became of him?"

Peter reached into the watch pocket of his trousers and came up with a small, silver pillbox. He opened it and picked out an orange pill and washed it down with his coffee.

"Aren't you feeling well?"

"I didn't get much sleep last night, and I'd like to make up for it now," he said. "If you'll excuse me." He reclined his seat and seemed to fall almost immediately to sleep.

Stone and Dino moved to another seating group and left him to it.

"He was surprisingly talkative," Dino said.

"Yes. It will be interesting to see how much of it is true." Stone thought about calling Lance now, but the aircraft's satphone was not a secure form of communication. He read the *Times* for a while, then reclined his seat and succumbed to a nap.

———

He did not awake until Julie came and brought his seat upright. "Landing at Teterboro in five minutes," she said. "Please remain on the aircraft, until customs and immigration come aboard and clear us." They touched down softly and taxied to Jet Aviation.

Clearing in was quick, and Dino's big SUV awaited them on the ramp. They offered Peter a lift into the city, but he said he had a car waiting.

"Where are you staying?" Stone called after him as he walked away, but an airplane nearby was starting its engines, and he appeared not to have heard.

Dino and Viv dropped Stone off at his house, and Fred was there to handle his luggage. Stone went straight upstairs to bed and resumed his nap.

28

S tone slept through the night and woke at his usual seven o'clock. He turned on *Morning Joe*, then the dumbwaiter bell rang and he went to get his breakfast tray and the *Times*. He had finished his breakfast and started on the newspaper when his iPhone rang. "Yes, Lance?"

"Scramble."

"Scrambled."

"I hear that our Peter traveled with you. What do you have for me?"

"I have a recorded conversation. An interrogation, really."

"Recorded on what?"

"My iPhone, from my jacket's breast pocket."

"Turn on the speaker, set it down, and play it for me. It will be recorded at this end."

Stone did as he was instructed; while Lance listened, he read the front page of the *Times*.

"Not bad," Lance said, when the recording had finished. "Why did you stop?"

"Peter stopped, then took an Ambien, I think. Shortly afterward he was unavailable."

"We'll check every word of it," Lance said, then hung up.

Stone had finished the newspaper and started on the crossword when he heard Holly's name mentioned.

"We've just heard that Holly Barker will hold a press briefing at ten AM from the State Department. Can this be an announcement?"

Probably not, Stone thought. He had heard nothing from her while he was gone, and Lance had not mentioned the investigation, either. He continued with the crossword, then showered, shaved, and dressed and was in his office in time to turn on CNN and watch Holly walk to the podium in the State Department auditorium, which was packed with press, cameras, and staff. She looked freshly made up and coiffed and was wearing a fashionable business suit with a skirt.

"Good morning," she said. "I am sad to tell you that this will be my last press appearance at this venue." A moan from her audience. "I had breakfast with the president this morning and handed her my resignation, effective at ten-thirty this morning." She glanced at her watch. "Pretty soon. I then informed her that I would be making this announcement and accepted her good wishes.

"I will be making a further announcement in a speech at the National Press Club at one o'clock this afternoon, so I will save my political comments until that time. For now, I will only say that from that hour, I will be a candidate for the Democratic nomination for President of the United States." That was followed by gasps of delight and applause and cheering. Holly smiled. "I can see you're glad to see me go."

"No, no!" they yelled.

"I am very happy to have this time to thank everyone in this building and in every foreign embassy and station for the hard work they have given their country during my time as secretary of state. You have all made me look good, and I thank you for that.

"Now I face about two and a half hours of unemployment before taking on the role of candidate. I wish it weren't too early to drink bourbon. Maybe later."

She strode from the podium with a wave, to sustained cheering and applause.

Stone was still breathing hard when his iPhone rang.

"Scramble," she said.

"Scrambled. I just heard your statement," Stone replied. "I'm thrilled for you."

"Thank you, kind sir."

"Where are you?"

"In a Secret Service tank, disguised as an SUV, on the way home to catch my breath before my big speech this afternoon. Secret Service protection will be seamless during the transition from office to office-seeking. I've gotta run."

"Wait a minute. What about the mole investigation?"

"It's over. Call Lance for details. I'll be in New York soon. I'll call you with my schedule." She hung up.

Stone's phone rang before he could put it down. "Yes?"

"Scramble."

"Scrambled."

"You were about to call me, so I thought I'd save you the trouble."

"Thank you. Holly tells me the mole investigation is over. What did you find?"

"Absolutely nothing. Marty's investigation says it was a red herring. Not even a whiff of anything real."

"I guess that's a relief, but I'd feel better if some guy were hanging by his heels in the cellar at Langley."

"That's always a lot of fun, but no need this time. We do have other things to discuss, though."

"Tell me."

"A preliminary check on what Peter told you on your pond crossing drew a blank on every single thing, up until he joined the *Paris Review* all those years ago. Fortunately, we had representation on that staff."

"Wait a minute. What about his family background?"

"Absolutely zip. No Cambridge birth certificate, no parents, no Groton, no Harvard. There *was* a girl named Ashley Dunham, and she was Howard Dunham's granddaughter, but the airliner she was taking back after that visit to Paris with Peter crashed shortly after takeoff from Orly, and there were no survivors."

"Holy shit," Stone muttered.

"Well, yes. Peter's first passport was issued for that trip, giving his birthplace as Cambridge. Now we're investigating the period of the *Paris Review* and Michelin employments and the trip to Russia. Georgi Arbatov was a real person and held the position Peter said he did, and the description of his broad contacts inside and outside the Soviet Union rings true. We'll be trying very hard to learn exactly how Peter spent his time during his month in the USSR."

"Let me guess: indoctrination and training."

"Very possibly, but so far, unproven. Where is he staying in New York?"

Stone confessed his failure to find out.

"That would have been helpful," Lance said, then hung up.

Joan was standing at his desk when Stone put down his phone. "Your mail, sir," she said, dropping a stack of magazines and catalogs on his desk. "Did you bring a package with you from Paris?"

"Gifts for everyone are over there," Stone said, pointing at a chair.

"Thank you sweetly, but that's not the sort of package I was thinking of. I was thinking female."

"I left with one, but came back without her. She jumped ship when a business opportunity raised its head."

"Good excuse," Joan said, then went back to her office.

Stone tackled his mail and messages.

S tone had finished lunch when his iPhone rang: a Paris number calling. "Hello?"

"Good afternoon to you," she said. "It's Tessa."

"And good evening to you."

"How was your flight back?"

"Flawless, thank you."

"I thought you might take the opportunity to get to know Peter better."

"I did take the opportunity, but the results were questionable."

"Surely your friend Lance could help with that."

"Not so much. At Teterboro I muffed the opportunity to find out where Peter is staying. A car met him."

"Oh, I can tell you that: he's at the Harvard Club. He's too cheap to stay at a hotel."

"Even when he's flush with cash?"

"I forgot about that. In that case, he'll be in a suite at the Pierre. He does that sort of thing when he's flush, or when somebody else is paying."

"Thank you, that narrows it down. What are you doing with yourself this week?"

"There's a big party tonight that I planned, then I will be idle."

"Then why don't you be idle in New York? I'll arrange a flight for you."

"That sounds irresistible," she said.

"Then don't resist."

"You win. There's a flight at two tomorrow." She gave him the flight number.

"My driver will meet you at JFK," Stone said. "Watch for a small man with a sign bearing your name. His name is Fred."

"Will do."

"Call me when you're inbound. We'll have dinner here, because you'll be tired."

"Oh, good. Then we can concentrate on you making me even more tired."

"That we can do." They said goodbye and hung up. Stone buzzed Joan.

"Yes, sir?"

"The package will be inbound tomorrow." He gave her the details and asked her to book Tessa in first class. "Have Fred meet her. Her name is Tessa Martindale."

"Certainly."

Stone hung up and called Dino.

"Bacchetti."

"You over jet lag?"

"Sure."

"Dinner at seven? Patroon."

"Okay. Viv has already left for Singapore."

"Then I'll book for two." They both hung up, then Stone called Lance. "Scramble."

"Scrambled."

"I have news: Peter Grant is likely staying at either the Harvard Club or the Pierre."

"What is your source?"

"Tessa Martindale, who seems to know him as well as anybody. It's more likely the Pierre, she says, because he's flush."

"I'll have him observed," Lance said, "and we'll see who he sees."

"I have nothing else."

"Bye." Lance hung up.

His duty done, Stone went upstairs for a nap, to deal with the last of his jet lag, then dressed comfortably for dinner.

Stone was on time, but Dino was early and half a drink ahead. The owner, Ken Aretsky, seated Stone. "How's the new airplane?" he asked.

"Awfully nice," Stone said, sliding into the booth. His drink arrived, concurrent with Ken's departure. "Did you tell him about the airplane?" Stone asked Dino.

"*Everybody* knows about the airplane, Stone. Get used to not being embarrassed because you can afford a Gulfstream."

"I'm working on that," Stone said. "Tessa's arriving tomorrow evening."

"What took you so long?"

"She's throwing one of her parties tonight."

"Then I guess you'll have to wait until tomorrow," Dino said. "Can you go that long without sex?"

"I'm not sure if that's an insult or a compliment."

"Neither. It's just a comment on your constitution, which is formidable."

"You probably have more sex than I do, Dino."

"When she's not in Singapore, or somewhere else exotic, she's demanding."

"Good for you."

"Keeps me in shape." Dino looked across the room. "Look who's here."

Peter Grant, in the company of an attractive woman, was being seated across the room.

Stone took the opportunity to call Lance, and they scrambled. "I thought you'd like to know that Peter Grant is dining at Patroon," Stone said.

"I know," Lance replied. "Do you see another couple entering?"

"Yes," Stone said, spotting two young people being seated.

"They're ours. Oh, and you were right about the Pierre. Bye." Lance hung up.

"The other couple that just came in belongs to Lance," he said to Dino.

"So Peter has grown a tail?"

"Yes. Tessa predicted he'd be at the Pierre."

"Newfound wealth is a great thing, isn't it?" Dino said.

"And he's making the most of it." Stone looked up to see another couple being seated with Peter and his date. "Now, who could that be?" he asked, half to himself.

"Lance will know in a couple of minutes," Dino replied.

The man appeared to be in his sixties, white-haired and well-dressed. His companion was too young to be his wife, so she probably was.

"Does he look Russian to you?" Stone asked.

"What does Russian look like? I mean, I know central casting Russian, but a real one?"

Stone stopped Ken Aretsky as he passed. "Ken, do you know the couple you just seated across the room?"

"The people with Peter Grant? No. Should I?"

"Did you hear him speak as you were seating him?"

"Yes."

"Any accent?"

"Southern," Ken said. "Charleston, I'd say."

"Is that in Russia?" Dino asked.

30

Tessa got in on schedule, and she took a few minutes before they met in Stone's study for drinks.

"What a nice room!" she said, as Stone handed her a vodka gimlet.

"Thank you."

"In fact, it's a nice house all over, from what I've seen."

"Thank you again."

"I don't think a woman did it," Tessa said. "Didn't your late wife have the decorator bug?"

"She did, but it was decorated before she moved in, and anyway, she had just exhausted her efforts in that regard in the building of a house in Virginia."

"Do you still own that?"

"No. Our son didn't want it, either, so I sold it."

"Why are you and Lance Cabot so interested in Peter Grant?" she asked, without preamble.

"I'm not, and I don't know why Lance is."

"That doesn't make any sense," she said.

"Perhaps Lance is interested because he's unaccustomed to not knowing everything about everybody."

"Well, surely, with that huge organization at his beck and call, he could know everything about anybody in a flash."

"Not when that person has spent half a lifetime erasing his past."

Tessa blinked. "You can tell me this is none of my business, if you like."

Stone obliged her. "This is none of your business—not that I think that will make the slightest difference."

"You're getting to know me pretty well," she said.

"And you, me. I didn't tell you I'd been married."

"I'm a curious person."

"That's putting it mildly."

"Does it offend you?"

"Not at all. My life is an open book, even if Peter's isn't."

"Why is the CIA after him?"

"I have no knowledge that they are. It's just that Lance is the only person I know who is more curious than you."

"Can I tell Peter that the CIA has no interest in him?"

"You can tell him anything you like, as long as you don't bring my name into it. I'm afraid that's a hard-and-fast rule if you and I are to remain friends. May I have your promise?"

"I don't like making promises," Tessa said.

"Because you might have to keep them?"

"Exactly."

"There's a flight back to Paris tomorrow, and you have a round-trip ticket."

"Oh, all right, I promise I won't talk to Peter about you."

"Thank you. I'll hold you to that."

"I can ask you questions about Lance, though, can't I?"

"Almost everything I know about Lance is reaped from my personal acquaintance with him. I have no knowledge how he operates or why he does what he does. If I get curious, I remind myself that what he does is a matter of national security, and I don't have a need to know, and you will be a happier person if you adopt that attitude."

"Is that a threat?"

"Certainly not."

"Then why will I be a happier person if I adopt your attitude?"

"Because you won't continually be wondering about Lance. Your mind will be free to be occupied by more pleasant thoughts, like what we are going to do to each other after dinner."

"So, if I should find myself thinking about anything to do with Lance, I should just think about sex?"

"A good policy, as long as it's sex with me."

"Do you object to my having sex with others?"

"You are a free woman. You may do anything you like."

He poured them another drink while she thought about that.

"And," she said, "I suppose you have the same freedom?"

"Of course. Would you deny me that?"

"Perhaps over the short term."

"I promise not to have sex with anybody but you—tonight."

Fred appeared in the doorway. "Dinner in ten minutes, sir."

"Thank you, Fred," Stone replied.

"You have an answer for everything, don't you?" Tessa asked.

"I'd better, when I'm with someone as curious as you."

"See what I mean?"

"I'm just trying to hold up my end of the conversation," Stone replied. "Later, I'll hold up your end."

"So to speak."

"So to speak."

Dinner arrived, and they worked their way through potato and leek soup, a rack of lamb, and apple pie à la mode.

After the meal, they took their brandy upstairs and playfully undressed each other.

Stone, as promised, held up her end and met her most urgent needs, then she did the same for him. They woke in the middle of the night for a repeat performance, then again after the sun rose.

"What are your plans for today?" Stone asked during breakfast.

"Shopping."

"Isn't there enough shopping in Paris?"

"It's different, somehow."

"I'll give you Fred and the car for the day," he said.

"How sweet of you!"

"It will give you somewhere to put the shopping bags."

tone arrived in his office to find a cream-colored envelope on his desk with his name written on it in beautiful calligraphy. He opened it and read an invitation to dinner from Peter Grant at a suite in the Pierre Hotel. He picked up the phone and buzzed Tessa.

"Talk fast."

"I've received an invitation to dinner from Peter Grant; any interest?"

"Peter's parties are always interesting."

"Then I'll accept."

"You do that, and I'll go shop for something stunning to wear."

"Good." Stone hung up and buzzed Joan. He read the RSVP number on the invitation. "Please accept for me, and mention that Tessa will be coming as well."

"Will do."

Stone's iPhone rang and he answered.

"Scramble."

"Scrambled."

"Peter Grant is throwing a dinner party at the Pierre this evening. I want you to be there."

"I have already accepted," Stone said.

"Are you taking a female?"

"I'm surprised to hear you ask," Stone replied. "You always know everything about me, Lance, sometimes before I do."

"It's Tessa, is it?"

"See?"

"Don't be a smart-ass; Tessa is perfect for the evening. She'll worm everything out of everybody she meets."

"Probably."

"Suggest to her that she ask everyone she meets how he or she met Peter."

"I don't think I'll have to suggest that."

"I want a list this time tomorrow," Lance said, then hung up.

"I got lucky at Ralph Lauren," she said, presenting herself to Stone. She looked gorgeous in the long black skirt and a black top with shiny, horizontal gold bands across it.

"You certainly did," Stone agreed.

They arrived at the Pierre only fashionably late and took the elevator to the floor marked PH.

"Looks as if Peter really splurged," Tessa said as they rode up. "There must be someone coming that he really wants to impress."

Tessa was right. As they stepped from the elevator car, past a burly man who looked like security, Stone spotted Yevgeny Chekhov across a fairly crowded room. "I can't wait to see the wine list," he said to Tessa.

"Looks like he wants to impress Mr. Chekhov over and over," she said.

"By the way," Stone said, "whenever you meet anyone new this evening, ask them how they met Peter."

"Did Lance Cabot tell you to tell me that?"

"Don't ask."

Stone snagged a couple of glasses of champagne from a passing waiter, then towed Tessa toward Chekhov.

"Ah, Stone," Chekhov said when he saw them. "And the lovely Tessa."

"Good evening, Yevgeny," Stone replied. "How long have you been in New York?"

Chekhov glanced at his watch. "About six hours," he said. "And you?"

"A couple of days."

"I rode his coattails," Tessa said, flashing him a smile.

"Nice place Peter has," Stone said.

"I suspect he rented it for the occasion," Chekhov said. "He's probably staying somewhere downstairs from here. Have you seen the view?" He indicated that they should explore the terrace.

The lamps in Central Park had already come on, and across Fifth Avenue the Plaza was bathed in floodlights. The faint echo of a police siren and a few horns floated up from the street.

"One doesn't get views like this in Moscow," Chekhov said, "unless one is at the top of one of those awful Stalinist apartment buildings."

"What brings you to New York, Yevgeny?" Stone asked, noting that his English had improved since their last meeting.

"Business," the Russian replied.

"I never asked you what sort of business you are in."

"This and that," Chekhov replied. "Whatever will turn a ruble."

"Do you have any particular interest in any particular field?"

"I'm interested in money," Chekhov replied, "especially dollars and euros."

"Once you've earned those, what do you invest them in?" Stone persisted.

"I'm interested in what will make them grow. I do quite a lot of lending, as long as the rates are good. I suppose you could say I'm something of a loan fish."

"I think you might mean loan shark."

"Ah, yes, that's the word. Do you have any borrowing requirements, Stone?"

"No, I manage to operate debt free, and I'd like to keep it that way."

"Too bad," Chekhov said. "I imagine that you are quite creditworthy."

"I suppose I am, but I haven't put my credit status to the test for quite some time."

"Then I will have to find other chickens to pick."

Stone and Tessa both laughed at that. "Pluck," Stone said. "Peter Grant, perhaps?"

"Not at the moment, but after he has squandered his newfound wealth on parties like this one and the one in Paris, I think I may feel certain that he will soon come calling."

"Is that his pattern?" Stone asked.

"It is."

"Tell me, if you haven't already: How did you come to meet Peter?"

"I met him a few years ago at a dinner party at the Kremlin."

"I suppose there is only one person who is the host there."

"Quite right. I was intrigued as to how an American adventurer had come to be acquainted with that host."

"What did you learn about that?"

"Neither Peter nor our host was amenable to the question, especially Peter, who exhibited fright when I asked it."

"And I thought you would know everything about Peter," Stone said.

"Oh, I do now, but not then." Chekhov caught sight of someone across the room and excused himself.

"I'll bet Lance is going to love that bit of gossip," Tessa said.

"It's not gossip when it's from the horse's mouth," Stone replied.

32

They wandered around for a half hour, chatting with whomever they came across, then found a comfortable sofa tucked in a corner of the living room and made themselves at home.

Stone handed her his pocket jotter and his pen. "Lance wants a list of everyone you meet and how that person met Peter."

"I can remember all that," she said, handing back the notebook.

Stone gave it to her again. "This will prevent your having to recite the list to Lance on the phone tomorrow morning."

She sighed and accepted the jotter, then started writing rapidly. "There," she said, "that should hold Lance for a while."

Stone read the list. "Where did you learn to write so fast and so legibly?"

"In school," she replied.

"What school?"

Tessa ignored the question and nodded toward the door, where the governor of New York was entering the room.

"Excellent," Stone said. "Now, as George Sanders said to Marilyn Monroe in that movie, 'Go do yourself some good.'"

Tessa rose and made her way through the crowd, where she

managed to collide with the governor. A conversation ensued, and she returned to the sofa. "Give me the jotter," she said, then sat down and wrote half a page.

Stone read over her shoulder. "The governor met Peter at a soccer match last year?"

"That's his story." She handed back the jotter.

"Where would he find a soccer match in New York?"

"At some place called Randall's Island," she replied. "Where is that?"

"In the middle of the East River," Stone replied. "That's the river to the east, not the one to the west, which is the Hudson River."

"I think I knew that. There's a soccer stadium there?"

"I'm not going to argue soccer geography with the governor," Stone said.

"Isn't there a Governors Island, too?"

"Yes, but that one comes under the purview of the federal government, not the state. It's much nicer than Randall's Island, though. That's where they train garbage collectors to do their work, or used to. I can't keep up with these things." Stone looked toward the door in time to see Bill Eggers enter. "Ah," he said, "there's someone worth talking to."

"Who is he?"

"My boss, or more accurately, the managing partner of the law firm in which I am a partner."

"I thought Lance Cabot was your boss."

Stone pulled her to her feet and guided her toward Eggers. "I keep telling you. I don't work for Lance, I just advise him on occasion."

"You seem to have done nothing else since I met you," Tessa said.

"Bill," Stone said, stopping him in his tracks, "I'd like to introduce you to my friend Tessa Martindale, who hails from across the Great Pond."

The two shook hands and exchanged greetings.

"Bill," Tessa asked, "where did you meet Peter Grant?"

"Who?" Eggers asked.

"Your host," Stone explained.

"Oh. My wife accepted the invitation, then she got mad at me about something or other and refused to come—this after I was already tuxedoed to the gills, so I decided to come on my own. Which one is Peter Grant?"

Stone spoke up. "See the Venus de Milo? Third male to her missing left."

"Looks familiar," Bill said.

"Think about it, Bill. Is he really familiar, or have you already had a couple of drinks?"

"Both, I think. I believe I shook his hand at a dinner at the Friars Club last night."

"That must have stamped him permanently on your frontal lobe."

"He spilled a drink on my other tuxedo," Eggers explained. "You don't forget people who do that."

"Did anyone pick your pocket while you were dealing with it?"

Eggers felt himself all over. "Nope, not unless they replaced my wallet, which is in its usual place. Is that Yevgeny Chekhov over there, talking to the redhead?"

"It is; how do you know him?"

"He had just been introduced to me by Grant, when he spilled the drink on me."

"Do you know who he is?"

"I did, vaguely, so I had my secretary look him up this morning. I believe he's someone important in the Soviet . . . Oops, what's it called now? The People's Republic of Russia?"

"The Russian Federation, I believe."

"One of their oligarchs, I think. They're a nasty bunch, aren't they?"

"Yes, but you'd better not let Chekhov hear you say that."

"I suppose not. I had a phone call from him this morning, but I didn't call him back."

"Why not?"

"Because he's a nasty piece of work."

"I think that's a reasonable description."

"How did you meet him?" Eggers asked.

"At a function very much like this one, in Paris. He asked me to lunch."

"Did you go?"

"Lance Cabot insisted," Stone replied.

"Then he must be a *really* nasty piece of work."

33

Somebody rang a little silver bell, and the guests began looking for their place cards among the tables in the dining room. Stone found himself sitting beside the redhead he had seen Chekhov talking to before dinner. Tessa was at another table, seated next to Chekhov. Peter Grant came in and sat on the other side of the redhead.

"Good evening, Stone," Peter said. "I'm sorry I didn't get to greet you and Tessa earlier."

"You were very busy, Peter, but good evening to you."

"Have you met Vanessa Baker?" Peter asked, referring to the redhead.

"I was just about to," Stone said, offering his hand. "I'm Stone Barrington."

Hers was cool, with long fingers, befitting her height. "How do you do?" she said, in a thoroughly American accent.

"Stone does very well," Peter interjected. "He's an important New York attorney."

"That's flattering," Stone said. "And like most flattery, not quite true."

"Well, Peter," she said, "Stone is modest."

"At times," Peter replied.

"And how do you earn your daily bread, Vanessa?" Stone asked, hoping to exclude Peter from the conversation.

"Funny you should ask," she replied. "I'm a baker."

Peter jumped in again. "Now it's Vanessa who's being modest," he said. "She owns a chain of bakeries around the city called Baker's Half Dozen."

"I've seen them," Stone said. "They always look inviting."

"That's what everyone says about Vanessa," Peter said.

"Thank you, Peter," Vanessa said. "Now, it's time for you to get to know the guest on your right."

Peter obediently turned to his other guest.

"Peter is just trying to be helpful," Vanessa said, "but he can be a pain in the ass sometimes."

"Do you have to get up at four o'clock in the morning to bake bread?" Stone asked.

"Fortunately not. I passed that chore on to others a few years ago."

"Then you don't have a good excuse for leaving this party early?"

"I don't need an excuse to leave a dull party," she replied. "I just walk out. But this promises to be an interesting dinner."

"I'll do what I can to help," Stone said.

Peter turned back toward her. "Oh, I forgot to mention that Stone works for the CIA, too."

"Please explain that, Stone," Vanessa said, "so I won't have to speak to Peter again."

"Once again, Peter exaggerates," Stone said. "I advise the director of the Central Intelligence Agency from time to widely separated time."

"And what sort of advice do you give him?"

"I'm afraid you'll have to ask the director that question, since I'm sworn to secrecy."

"How disappointing."

"Oh, only on subjects related to the Agency. Otherwise, I'm an open book."

"I very much doubt that," she said. "You look quite mysterious to me."

Stone laughed. "No one has ever said that to me before."

"Give me your sixty-second bio," she said.

"Born Greenwich Village, attended the local schools, including NYU and its law school. Passed on the practice of law in favor of becoming a police officer—until I took a bullet in the knee, and the department used that as an excuse to invalid me out. Old law school buddy came to the rescue and offered me a job with his firm; the CIA asked me for advice. I think that brings me up to date. Your turn."

"All right. Born on the Upper East Side, year classified. Attended the local schools, then one on the Upper West Side called Columbia. Grandfather died and left an old family business, a bakery. I took it over and built it into Baker's Half Dozen."

"That was skimpy," Stone said. "I want more."

"Then you'll have to do it over dinner on another occasion," she replied, fishing a card out of a tiny handbag.

Stone reciprocated. "I'll call," he said.

"I'll count on it."

"You're neglecting me," a woman's voice said from behind him.

Stone turned to find a beautiful woman, probably in her mid-sixties, seated on his other hand; he introduced himself.

"I'm Betty Baker," she replied. "You'll have to be nice to me—I'm Vanessa's mother."

"I'll be very nice to you, and not just because you're Vanessa's mother."

"Well," she said, "this has suddenly become a promising evening." She talked so well that Stone never got around to Vanessa again. Not until they moved into the living room for coffee and brandy did he lose Betty.

Tessa materialized beside him. "I was surprised to see you talking to the silver fox instead of the redhead," she said.

"The silver fox was captivating. How was your evening beside Mr. Chekhov?"

"Somewhat less than captivating."

"Then you'll have to write down some notes for me to pass on to Lance Cabot tomorrow."

"I'll do that, but not until tomorrow," she said. "Mr. Chekhov has taken up quite enough of my time for this evening."

Stone looked over her shoulder to see Vanessa Baker making her way toward the front door, in company with her mother. They both winked at him.

34

S tone was awakened the following morning by a scratching
noise, which turned out to be the sound of a pencil on paper.
Tessa handed him the page. "For Lance," she said.

Stone rang for breakfast, then turned his attention to her report. "Splendid," he said. "And what school taught you to apply
pencil to paper so beautifully?"

She scrunched down beside him, fondled his genitalia, and said,
"I believe we have time before breakfast to put this to use, and it
appears to agree with me."

Stone could not deny her. They were just reaching a climax
when the dumbwaiter bell rang.

"What exquisite timing," Tessa said.

"And, once again, I ask you: How did you learn to take notes so
rapidly and perfectly?"

She heaved a sigh as he got out of bed to retrieve their tray. "Oh,
all right: I attended a language school, and I spoke the language so
badly that they taught me a new skill instead."

"What was the language?" he asked.

"Russian."

"And who . . ."

She held up a finger to stop him. "Sorry, I'm eating now." She took a big bite of muffin and chewed thoughtfully.

Stone shaved, showered, gave Tessa a kiss, and went down to his office, depositing Tessa's notes on Joan's desk with instructions to scan and e-mail them to Lance Cabot.

He had hardly sat down at his desk when his iPhone buzzed.

"I'm scrambled," Stone said.

"These are perfectly beautiful notes," Lance said.

"I thank you on behalf of the note taker."

"Ah, it was the lovely Tessa, wasn't it?"

"I cannot deny that. I think I'm beginning to see at whose language school she learned to do that."

"It's a sort of backup skill we teach to those who are not born linguists," Lance said. "I wish we taught it to all our students, because then I could read their reports so much more easily."

"Have you found anything of interest therein?" Stone asked.

"Everything," Lance said. "So much so that I am going to have to deprive you of Tessa's company with immediate effect."

"Why would you do that?"

"Because she is needed elsewhere, and my need trumps yours."

"Why didn't you just tell me she was one of yours?"

"It was a need-to-know thing," Lance replied. "Now Tessa has a need to travel, though I know you'll miss her."

"When can I have her back?" Stone asked.

"Perhaps soon, perhaps not."

"Did you learn the purpose of last evening's dinner?"

"I did, and it was the same purpose as the Paris dinner."

"When speaking to Chekhov, I divined that he was somewhat less enthralled with Peter and his entertainments than before."

"Some people just don't wear well," Lance said. "And Peter is, apparently, one of them."

"I agree," Stone said. "There isn't much there. Don't order me to accept any more of his invitations."

"We'll see." Lance hung up as he often did, unceremoniously.

Tessa appeared in the office doorway, closely followed by Fred, with her luggage on a cart. "I hope you've spoken to Lance," she said.

"I have."

"Oh, good, then I won't have to explain why I have to leave."

"I did not know until my conversation of a moment ago that you were subject to Lance's orders."

"It was a secret," she said.

"For how long?"

She eyed the ceiling while counting on her fingers. "Let's see. It was four—no, five years ago. I needed the money at the time. Now I do it because it's fun."

"I have not yet discovered that facet of Lance's personality."

"He grows on you." She came over to his desk and planted a lush and lingering kiss upon his lips. "I fly," she said, and she pretty much did. "I'll send Fred home soon," she called over her shoulder, then they were both gone.

Stone waited for a count of about twelve before rising and taking the elevator to the top floor, where he found Vanessa Baker's card in the pocket of last night's dinner suit. He sat down on the bed and dialed her number.

She answered on the first ring. "I thought you'd never call," she said.

"I see your caller ID is working."

"Just fine."

"Dinner?"

"Does it matter which night?"

"I was thinking tonight," he said.

"Funny, so was I. I have a thing earlier in the evening. May we meet at the restaurant?"

"As long as it's Patroon, on East 46th Street. May I send my car for you?"

"Oh, yes, you may. It's supposed to rain."

"Where and when?"

"Isn't that a song?"

"You're thinking of 'Where or When,' Rodgers and Hart."

"You're right. I'll be at 570 Park Avenue at, let's see, seven forty-five. I'll be standing under the awning, keeping dry. What sort of car?"

"A Bentley Flying Spur. I'll see you at Patroon at eight."

"Done." She hung up.

Stone asked Joan to book the table, then he got Tessa's notes and read them. Lance was right; her precise handwriting made them easy to digest.

Stone arrived at Patroon in a cab at the stroke of eight, just as Fred pulled up and assisted Vanessa Baker from the rear seat. She passed from his umbrella to Stone's. Then they went inside, checked their rain gear, and were shown to Stone's usual table.

"What would you like to drink?" Stone asked Vanessa.

"It feels like a brown whiskey evening," she said.

"Bourbon?"

She nodded. "Excellent."

Stone ordered Knob Creek for both of them. While they waited for delivery Stone asked her, "Tell me, do you work for the CIA?"

"No," she replied. "I don't believe they're in the baking business."

"I'm relieved to hear it," he replied, as their glasses were set down. They clinked them and drank.

35

They sat and watched the headwaiter, Stefan, work his magic with egg yolks, olive oil, and anchovies, whipped with a wooden spoon, tossed with romaine lettuce and croutons and dished out as Caesar salad. Then they began to munch.

"I love this," Vanessa said.

"So do I."

"So where has the lovely young lady from last evening gone?" she asked.

"She comes, she goes, on her own whim or that of others," he replied. "She doesn't ask my permission or offer explanations. Where has your mother gone?"

"At this moment, she has a dinner date with one of her fellas."

"You make them sound like a herd."

"They practically are. She doesn't have many nights off."

"I take it your father is not around."

"She kicked him out years ago. He lives on the proceeds of his share of the bakeries."

"I enjoyed Betty's company last night, though it deprived me of yours."

"Well, we're making up for that now, aren't we?"

They had finished their salads by the time their Dover sole arrived and was boned and served, along with a firm, crisp Puligny-Montrachet.

"How did you come to be at the party last night?" Stone asked her.

"Betty invited me to be her date," Vanessa replied.

"Then how did Betty come to be there?"

"Peter invited her and a date. Everybody else was busy, I guess."

"And how did Betty become acquainted with Peter?"

"She knew him as a younger man, when he lived in New York."

"What did Peter do with himself in those days?"

"The same thing he does now."

"Which is?"

"Nobody seems to know, certainly not Betty. If a man is handsome and a little bright, that's all she needs to know." She took a swig of her wine and smiled her approval. "I'm more demanding," she said.

"Then once again, I'm flattered."

"I knew you were going to be smart when I saw you across the room," she said. "That's why I moved my place card next to yours."

"What made you think I'd be smart?"

"It was the way you were talking to that very strange Russian," she said. "You appeared . . . skeptical."

"Oh, I am very skeptical of Comrade Chekhov," Stone replied.

"He, on the other hand, seems attracted to you."

"I think I can explain that," Stone said.

"Please do, unless you're going to tell me you're gay."

"No. Not very long ago I helped Mr. Chekhov make a great deal of money. Not directly. He invested in a company I owned, and there was an IPO. You know what that is."

"An initial public offering. Of course I know. I had one of my own two years ago."

"Congratulations. What Chekhov wants from me is a tip or two on another stock, and I have denied him that—and Chekhov is unaccustomed to being denied."

"I'm relieved to hear that it's not your body we're talking about."

"I believe I answered that question. Do you wish further proof?"

"Well, not in this restaurant," she replied. "Perhaps later?"

"I'll do what I can."

She laughed. "And how did you meet Mr. Chekhov?"

"At one of Peter's dinner parties in Paris."

"Were you there recently?"

"A few days ago."

"I wish I had been there."

"So do I. Perhaps one day soon I'll invite you to go."

"I'll look forward to it. What brought you back?"

"Well, occasionally, I have to appear to practice law. My firm expects it."

"Which firm?"

"Woodman & Weld."

"Was Bill Eggers the man who gave you a job when you stopped being a policeman?"

"He was. We were classmates in law school."

"They did the legal work on my IPO."

"How's your stock doing?"

"It's trebled since the day we rang the bell downtown."

"Congratulations again."

"This fish is marvelous," she said, taking another bite. "Is Peter Grant mixed up in something illegal?"

"Why do you ask?"

"Because I googled Mr. Chekhov when I got home last night, and the results were not edifying."

"Peter seemed to arrange things for his pleasure in Paris, and now in New York."

"Do you mean he's pimping for Chekhov?"

"Possibly. Or perhaps he just invites him to dinners where there are women, then lets him fend for himself. I don't think that's illegal."

"Do you think Chekhov is doing something illegal?"

"I expect so. Russian oligarchs don't get to be oligarchs any other way."

"Do you know what it is that he does?"

"Anything that involves money, to hear him tell it."

"And you've heard him tell it?"

"In small doses. Peter arranged a lunch at the Russian embassy, so that Chekhov could poke around for tips. I found him distasteful then, and nothing has changed since."

"I'm relieved to hear it," Vanessa said. "I was afraid you might be involved with him in some way. But now that we've established that you are not, will you invite me to your home for a nightcap? I want to see where you live."

"Certainly," Stone said, lifting a finger for the check.

The rain had stopped by the time they got to Turtle Bay, and they were able to enter through the front door instead of the garage.

Stone pressed the master light switch as they entered, and the living room lights came on.

"Very nice," she said, "and I'll bet you decorated it yourself."

"I did."

"It's very masculine, but comfortable."

"The bar is in my study, to your right." Stone led her in, lit the fire, and poured them each a cognac. She sat down in the middle of the sofa and patted the cushion next to her.

Stone sat. "I believe I offered you further proof of my sexuality," he said.

"I don't need proof," Vanessa said, "but don't let that stop you."

36

tone awoke a little before seven to find Vanessa gone from his bed; no note. He picked up the phone and ordered breakfast for himself, then went to the door to retrieve the *New York Times* and took it back to bed. He read the first section carefully and timed it for completion as breakfast arrived with the ring of the bell from the dumbwaiter.

He brought the tray back to his bed, set it on his lap, and ate, switching on the TV as he did so. Nothing of any consequence there. He finished his breakfast, carried the tray back to the dumbwaiter, and pressed the button for the kitchen. Then, as he turned back toward the bed, he saw something out of place: a woman's shoe just inside the bathroom door. Vanessa would not have left wearing only one shoe, he reflected. He walked toward the guest bathroom, and as he did, a foot, shoeless, came into view. He ran the remaining steps.

Vanessa, wearing her dress from the night before, was lying, crumpled, on the bathroom floor, her head against the bathtub.

Stone had seen a lot of corpses back in his NYPD days, and he knew immediately that she was dead. He felt for a pulse at her wrist and neck and got nothing. Her skin was cool to the touch.

Stone went back into the bedroom to call Dino, then stopped himself. Dino didn't like to be called first. He dialed 911, reported a woman deceased, and asked for the police, an ambulance, and the medical examiner, then he hung up and called Dino's cell.

"Bacchetti."

"It's Stone. There's a female, deceased, lying on my bathroom floor."

"Have you touched anything?"

"The bathroom floor, with my bare feet, and her wrist and neck with my fingers. No pulse, and she's cooler than normal."

"Did you call 911?"

"Yes."

"I'll be there in twenty minutes." Dino hung up.

A few minutes later the doorbell rang on his telephone. "Yes?"

"NYPD. You reported a death?"

"I'll buzz you in. Take the elevator to the fifth floor, then down the hall to the rear of the house. The bedroom door will be open." He pressed the front-door button then realized he was naked and went to his bathroom for a robe and slippers.

"Hello?" a voice called.

"Hello, coming." Stone stepped out of the bathroom and found two uniforms standing in the doorway. "There's a bathroom behind you. She's in there." While the two policemen investigated, Stone got into some clothes, then sat on the end of the bed and waited for them.

The two cops came out, and the older of the two produced a notebook and did the talking. "Your name?"

"Stone Barrington."

"Familiar," the man said.

"I'm retired NYPD, 19th Precinct."

"Ah. Her name?"

"Vanessa Baker."

"You know a next of kin?"

"Her mother, Betty Baker."

"Address and phone?"

"I don't know. If Vanessa's handbag is in the bathroom, it might be on her phone."

The younger cop went into the bathroom and came out holding a black alligator handbag and a business card. "I've got an office number and phone for the deceased."

"Probably too early for anyone to answer there," Stone said, checking his watch. "It's seven-fifty-five."

"Tell me about last night," the elder cop said.

"She had drinks with somebody at 570 Park Avenue. I sent my car for her and she met me at Patroon, a restaurant on East 46th Street. We had dinner, then came back here for a nightcap. After that we came up here and spent the night together."

"She looks dressed to go," the cop said.

"At some point she got out of bed without waking me and, I guess, went into the bathroom to dress. I didn't find her until about seven-forty, then I called 911."

"Did you call anyone else?" the cop asked.

"He called me," a voice said from the bedroom door. Dino was standing there, leaning against the jamb. "Carry on, Officer."

"Yes, Commissioner," he said with a gulp. "Mr. Barrington, did you touch anything in the bathroom?" he asked.

"The floor with my feet, her wrist and neck, while looking for a pulse."

"Did you administer CPR?"

"I've seen a lot of corpses in my time, and I knew that wouldn't help. It would also have disturbed your crime scene, if I'd moved the body."

The doorbell rang again.

"I'll get it," Dino said. He picked up the phone and told them to come upstairs, then pressed the button.

The cop turned to his partner. "Did you see any marks on the corpse?"

"A contusion on the right temple," he replied. "Looks like she collapsed and struck her head on the bathtub. There's a smudge of makeup on the porcelain. Also, she threw up in the toilet but didn't flush."

"That's a break," the cop said.

Dino brought in two men with a stretcher and another with a medical bag. "In there," he said to them, pointing at the bathroom.

"Is your crime scene secure?" the ME asked the cop.

"Yes." He and his partner stood aside to allow the ME to enter the bathroom. "She vomited," said the young cop to him. "Check out the toilet."

"How long have you known the deceased?" the cop asked Stone.

"I met her the night before last at a dinner party at the Pierre Hotel."

"Who was the host?"

"Peter Grant, who is staying at the hotel."

"Did he introduce you to the deceased?"

"Sort of. She told me last night that she moved her place card next to mine. Her mother was on my other side."

The cop droned on with his questions, as if reading from a script. Stone looked at Dino, and he nodded, indicating his approval of the interrogation.

"Anything you'd like to know, Commissioner?" the cop asked.

"Where did you have dinner?"

"At Patroon."

"What did you both have to eat?"

"We both had the Caesar salad, the Dover sole, and a bottle of Puligny-Montrachet."

"Did you have a drink here, later?"

"We both had a cognac from the same bottle. It's on the coffee table in my study."

"I'll get a sample," the ME said, then left the room.

"Did you put anything in her food or drink?" Dino asked.

"Certainly not," Stone replied.

"Officer," Dino said, "I don't think you'll need to arrest Mr. Barrington. I'll vouch for him."

The body was removed on a gurney, under a sheet, then the crime scene specialists showed up and processed the bathroom and the study.

"You got some coffee?" Dino asked.

"Downstairs."

They went to the study; the cognac bottle was gone. Dino sat down. "Is there anything else you want to tell me? Just bet-ween us?"

"Not a thing," Stone said.

"No suspect in your mind?"

"No."

"Who was at the party?"

"The host, the girl and her mother, and about forty other peo-ple. Including Yevgeny Chekhov."

Dino's eyebrows went up. "That guy would be a suspect for any murder in any city."

"No doubt."

"I was surprised when you came back from your lunch with him still alive."

"He was talking to Vanessa when I arrived, but she told me dur-ing dinner that she was repelled by him."

"Maybe repelling wasn't his only crime. Did you see her leave the party?"

"Yes, she left with her mother, whose name is Betty Baker."

"I've got to get to the office. You want to do the honors?"

"I'll track her down," Stone said.

37

When Stone got to his office, Joan was waiting for him. "Who left the house on the gurney?" she asked.

"A woman of my acquaintance—you don't know her. Call the headquarters of a chain of bakeries called Baker's Half Dozen, and see if you can locate Mrs. Betty Baker at the office or at a home number. You can say that it's a personal matter and urgent."

"Right," Joan said. Shortly she buzzed him. "Mrs. Baker on one."

Stone picked up the phone. "Betty? It's Stone Barrington."

"Oh, Stone, what a nice surprise to hear from you."

"I'm afraid I call with bad news."

"Oh, God, is it something to do with Vanessa?"

"It is. We had dinner at a restaurant last night, then she asked to see my house, and we came back for a drink. She ended up staying the night, and sometime later, while I was asleep, she got up and dressed. I found her in the bathroom this morning. She had apparently fallen and struck her head on the bathtub. She did not survive the accident."

There was a moment's silence. "Where did they take her?"

"To the city morgue. I'll have them contact you when her body is ready to be released." He asked for her contact numbers; she thanked him and hung up.

Joan buzzed him. "The medical examiner is on line two."

Stone knew the man from his cop days, when he had been an assistant in the morgue. He picked up the phone. "Dave?"

"Good morning, Stone."

"How are you?"

"Let's leave the pleasantries for the moment. I have some interesting news for you."

"All right."

"I came into the office a few minutes ago, and a morgue assistant was waiting in my office. He had been on duty when a DOA came in, brought from your residence."

"Yes."

"He had a brief look at her, then covered the body and logged her in. A minute or two later a movement caught his eye, and he turned to see her arm dangling from the table." The ME paused.

"Go on, Dave."

"It struck him that her color was pink, where it had been dead white a moment before that. He went to the table, checked for a pulse at the wrist and neck—and found one. He confirmed it with a stethoscope, then he called Bellevue and asked for the EMTs and a doctor. The short story is: she's alive, but not conscious."

"Dave, this isn't some sort of bizarre morgue joke, is it?"

"I'm telling you true, Stone. Bellevue has her hooked up to the equipment and is trying to revive her."

"Thank you, Dave, I'll let her family know." He hung up and buzzed Joan. "Get Betty Baker on the phone—on her cell, if you have to—and pronto."

"Yes, boss." A moment later she buzzed. "Got her."

Stone picked up the phone. "Betty?"

"Yes, Stone, what is it? I have arrangements to make."

"Where are you?"

"In my car, on the way home."

"Go to Bellevue Hospital instead, to the emergency room. Vanessa has shown signs of life, and they're trying to revive her."

"Good God," she said quietly.

"Do you know where Bellevue is?"

"My driver does."

Stone gave her his number. "Please call me, when you know more."

"Stone?"

"Yes?"

"Will you meet me there? I'm going to need help with this."

"I'll be there in fifteen minutes," Stone said. He hung up, got into his jacket, and went into Joan's office. "Call the director of emergency medicine at Bellevue and remind him that they have a Vanessa Baker in their ER. Tell him her mother and an attorney are on the way there."

"Will do."

Stone hung up and buzzed Fred.

"Yes, sir?"

"I need the car ten minutes ago," Stone said.

Stone arrived at the hospital and read the directory on the wall. The director of emergency medicine was a William Golding, MD.

Stone went to the emergency room desk and got a woman's attention. "My name is Stone Barrington. I have to see Dr. Golding immediately—he's expecting me."

She spoke into the phone, then hung up. "He'll be here directly."
A moment later a curtain was swept aside, and a stout man in his
shirtsleeves looked around the waiting room and his eye fell on
Stone. "Are you Barrington?"

"Yes," Stone said.

"This way." Golding strode to an examination room with Stone
in tow, then closed the door behind him. "Do you have any idea
what's going on here?" he asked.

"She died, or I thought she did, in a bathroom in my house. The
authorities were called, and she was pronounced, in the presence
of the police commissioner, who is a friend of mine. A few minutes
ago I got a call from David Pelly at the morgue who told me she
was alive. I came right over, and her mother, Mrs. Betty Baker, is
on her way."

"Can you deal with the mother until I get this under control?"
Golding asked.

"All right. We'll be in the waiting room."

"I'll leave word at the desk to have both of you taken to my office."

Golding left, and Stone went back to the waiting room, in time
to intercept Betty.

"Where is she?" Betty asked.

"They're working on her now. No news, yet."

A nurse appeared at Stone's elbow. "Mr. Barrington, Mrs. Baker,
please follow me."

They were led to a fairly large, well-decorated office down a hallway. "Dr. Golding will be with you as soon as he can. Please have a seat."

They sat down on a sofa and waited, not talking much.

A half hour later, Golding came into the room, closing the door behind him, and introduced himself to Betty Baker.

"Mrs. Baker, Vanessa is alive and breathing on her own, which is very good news, but she is not yet conscious. This may be attributed to when she struck her head on the bathtub, or there could be a drug involved."

"My daughter didn't take drugs," Betty said.

Golding nodded. "Her X-rays showed no skull fracture, and that's good. What we can do now is to wait for her toxicology screen to come back and make her as comfortable as possible. If you like, you may use this office to wait, but I can't promise you that she will revive quickly, perhaps not even today. It might be best if you returned to your home, and I will contact you personally when I have something to report."

"That might be best, Betty," Stone said. "You'll be more comfortable. Or, if you prefer, you may come to my house and wait there. I'm in Turtle Bay."

Betty stood up. "I'll go home," she said. Stone followed her to the emergency entrance, where her car and his were waiting. "We'll speak later," she said, and got into her car and was driven away.

Stone went home and into his office.

Joan came in. "Can you tell me what's going on?"

"What, you didn't listen to my calls?"

"You know very well that I don't do that, unless . . . unless there's a very good reason to."

"I had a woman here last night who, while getting dressed in the guest bathroom, fell, struck her head on the tub, and appeared to be dead. The EMTs came, and the ME pronounced her, and she was taken to the morgue. A little later she began to move around, scaring a morgue assistant half to death, and now she's at Bellevue, breathing but still not awake. I await further news."

"Holy shit," Joan muttered. "Oh, sorry about that." She went back to her office.

Ten minutes later she buzzed him. "Dino on one."

Stone picked up the phone. "Yeah?"

"Jesus, can't you do anything right? You sent a living woman to the morgue?"

"Listen, pal, you were there, and you didn't throw yourself across her body to stop it. She was pronounced, for God's sake."

"Yeah, that's what they all say."

"All of who?"

"People who don't know how to take a pulse. I've had her mother on the phone, demanding to have you arrested."

"On what charge?"

"She was a little incoherent about that."

"I'm not surprised. I didn't send her to the morgue. Officials of the City of New York did that, and in the presence of the police commissioner! If she sues, I'm in the clear. You, not so much." Stone hung up, steaming.

38

Late in the afternoon, Stone called Dr. Golding at Bellevue.

"Yes, Mr. Barrington?"

"Any change?"

"Nothing startling. She's had a little eyelid flutter, and when that happened, a small increase in her pulse."

"It sounds like she could be trying to wake up," Stone said.

"You could interpret it that way, or a doctor—we have a lot of them around here—could justifiably say it was just low-level brain activity. That's my bet."

"What kind of odds do you give her?"

"One chance in fifty, and that's optimistic."

"What did her EEG say?"

"Low-level brain activity."

"Oh."

"Yeah. Her mother called. She's planning a welcome-home party."

"Well, she's a mother, isn't she?"

"Yeah. If I were in Vanessa's shape, my mother would be force-feeding me chicken soup."

"Thank you, Doctor; I hope for better news."

"Me, too. Though I so look forward to being sued."

"What for? She had already been through the worst before you got her. I'd take your case in a heartbeat—so to speak."

"Thanks, I feel so much better now. Bye." He hung up.

Joan buzzed him. "Dino on one."

"What?" Stone said.

"You sound terrible; did she die again?"

"Not yet, but Bellevue isn't optimistic."

"I'm sorry I yelled at you earlier."

"Why? How is that different from all the other times you've yelled at me?"

"I'll buy dinner—P.J. Clarke's, at seven. That'll cheer you up."

Stone was walking out of the house when his cell phone rang. "Hello?"

"It's Bill Golding, at Bellevue; there's news."

"What news?"

"I've got to get out of here before the media starts breaking my office door down. Can I buy you a drink?"

"I'm on my way to P.J. Clarke's now; meet me there."

"Give me a few minutes. I've got to report this to the police."

"You can take care of that at Clarke's. I'm having dinner with the cop in charge."

"See you in fifteen," Golding said, then hung up.

Dino was already at the bar, as the bartender set down two drinks. Stone grabbed one and sniffed it. "This one's yours," he said, handing it to Dino and grabbing the other.

They both took a heavy swig.

Stone looked over his shoulder to see Golding entering the place. They shook hands, and Stone introduced him to Dino. The headwaiter was beckoning to them.

"What are you having?" Stone asked.

"A double Talisker, rocks." The bartender overheard that and grabbed the bottle. "Send it to the table," Stone said, then led Golding and Dino to the back room. "Another chair," he said to the headwaiter.

Stone waited until everybody was seated and Golding's drink had been delivered and he had had a sip. "What's going on, Bill?"

"Is this guy your cop?"

"This is Dino Bacchetti."

"He's *the* cop, isn't he? You mentioned that he was present for the cockup."

"I was an innocent bystander," Dino said. "I never took her pulse." He jerked a thumb at Stone. "He did, though."

"Do you have any medical training, Stone? Were you qualified to pronounce her?"

"I was a homicide detective for many years, mostly with Dino for a partner. After a few dozen corpses, I caught on to the symptoms of death. Now, what's happened?"

"Her tox screen came back," Golding said. "She was poisoned."

"With what?"

"Have you been reading the papers about the death of the two former KGB agents in Britain, who were murdered by their former schoolmates?"

"I have."

"We've been on the phone for the past two hours talking to the people who dealt with that, and we're pretty sure it's the same drug. Knowing what it is gives her a better chance of recovery."

"Have you told her mother?"

Golding shook his head. "I couldn't, until I reported it to the police."

"Consider it reported," Dino said. "You'd better call her, before she hears about it on TV."

"Excuse me a moment," Golding said. He left the table, then came back for his drink. "I'm going to need this. Order me a steak, rare, and another drink." He left the room.

Dino got out his phone and pressed a button. "Find Johnny Goode," he said, then hung up.

"Who's he?" Stone asked.

"He's kind of our specialist detective in poisonings," Dino replied.

"I didn't know you had a specialist in poisonings."

"We don't, that's why I said 'kind of.'" Dino's phone rang, and he picked it up. "Johnny B.," he said. "I've got something for you. You know the people in England the KGB poisoned? There have been three or four. Right. We've got a lady at Bellevue, name of Vanessa Baker. We think she took whatever they took. I want you to call MI-5 and find out everything you don't already know about those poisons, particularly how long they take to take effect. Yeah, I know it's the middle of the night there. Wait until they're up, then call me back when you're our resident genius. You'll be the lead detective on the case." Dino hung up. "Johnny B. Goode is on it."

"That's really his name?"

"Not the 'B.' part, but everybody calls him that, anyway."

"Of course they do."

"Or they wouldn't be cops," Dino said.

"This is going to be a tough case," Stone said.

"I think it'll be a lot easier if Vanessa starts walking and talking," Dino replied.

"Out of the four cases in England, so far," Stone said, "only one of them is walking and talking."

"I've had worse odds," Dino said.

"Good for you."

Bill Golding arrived back at the table with an empty glass in his hand. "I need this one," he said, grabbing the fresh one.

ill Golding attacked the slab of meat that was before him.
"Vanessa continues to show signs of recovery," he said. "Her
mother is with her, and I'm glad I'm here."

"Who's treating her?" Stone asked.

"We've got a poison team, and they're on it, but they've
never seen anything like this—a poison that takes twenty-four
to seventy-two hours to act. That's what the literature, such as it
is, says."

"Let's count backward," Dino said. "Stone, you found her dead,
sort of, at what time?"

"Around seven-forty AM."

"Did you see her the evening before?"

"Yes, I did."

"And the big dinner was the night before that?"

"Right, and she was at another dinner the night before that."

"Then," Golding said, "the big dinner two nights ago looks
good. Forty-eight hours, or so, have passed since then, and it was
twelve hours ago that you discovered her unconscious in your
bathroom. She had vomited, as I recall."

"That's right."

"That may have saved her life by getting rid of some of the poison."

"I sat between Vanessa and her mother," Stone said, "and she ate what we all ate."

"How did you happen to be seated in that position?" Dino asked.

"I sat where my place card was. Vanessa told me she had moved hers next to mine."

"Then where did she move it from?"

"I don't know."

"What did you all have for dinner?" Golding asked.

"Breast of chicken in a cream sauce and flavored with brandy, potatoes au gratin, haricots verts."

"Starter?"

"A slab of seared foie gras," Stone said.

"Dessert?"

"Crème brûlée."

"And what were you all drinking?"

"A French burgundy. There were two bottles on the table."

"Dessert wine?"

"A sauterne. I don't know which one."

"Coffee?"

"Later, in the living room. Vanessa and her mother didn't stay for coffee. I saw them leave."

"Do you know if she had a drink before dinner?" Golding asked.

Stone thought about it. "When I got to the party, I saw a Russian of my acquaintance standing with her, and they both had drinks in their hands. The Russian's was clear—vodka, I guess. Hers was whiskey-colored."

"Very good."

"He didn't mention that the Russian was ex-KGB," Dino pointed out, "and has an unsavory reputation."

"Right," Stone said. "He would know people who could arrange a poisoning."

"Who was in the kitchen?" Golding asked.

"A caterer, I guess. I never went into the kitchen."

"How many people at this party?"

"Forty, maybe."

"My money's on the Russian," Dino said.

"Mine, too," Stone replied. "I can't prove it. Can you?"

"Not yet."

Golding put down his steak knife and polished off his drink. "I've got to go home before my wife divorces me," he said. "Can I contribute to dinner?"

"You already have," Dino said "Good luck at the hospital and with your wife."

Golding shook their hands and departed.

"Well, we have a clearer picture of events now," Dino said.

"I'm glad you do," Stone replied. "I don't have a fucking clue."

"We need a motive," Dino said.

"We certainly do. Again, I'm clueless."

"Why would someone like Chekhov poison somebody at a big dinner party?"

"Cover," Stone said. "Lots of other suspects."

"In Paris, you said this Peter Grant guy kowtows to Chekhov, right?"

"Right."

"Does he kowtow enough to commit murder on Chekhov's instructions?"

"One more thing I don't know," Stone said.

"Check with Lance, will you?"

"First thing tomorrow," Stone said.

Stone was having breakfast the following morning when his iPhone rang. "I'll scramble," he said. "Done."

"What's this I hear about a poisoning?" Lance asked.

"Somebody was poisoned," Stone said.

"In your bathroom?"

"Twenty-four to forty-eight hours before my bathroom," Stone replied. "That's what her doctor reckons, anyway."

"Was Chekhov present?"

"In my bathroom?"

"At the dinner where she ingested the poison."

"Yes."

"Then he's your principal suspect."

"Funny, that's what Dino and I thought."

"Why hasn't Dino arrested him?"

"Dino needs evidence for an arrest. He's funny that way. Anyway, Chekhov's likely got a diplomatic passport. If he does, Dino can't even question him without the Russian ambassador's permission."

"Which will not be forthcoming, of course."

"I wouldn't be surprised if Chekhov has already left the country," Stone said.

"For where?"

"Anywhere he likes, I should think."

"Do you know how he was transported to New York?"

"Private airplane. He had one in Paris."

"I'll have a look taken at private flights. How's the girl doing?"

"Last night, her eyelids were fluttering. I've had no reports today."

"She's lucky to be alive."

"She may not be, for all I know."

"Call somebody and find out the latest," Lance said.

"As soon as everybody has time to get to work."

"I'm at work," Lance replied.

"Great, then you call somebody, Lance. I'm still having break-fast." Stone hung up.

Stone got himself together, then had Fred drive him to Bellevue. He took the elevator to the sixth floor and went to Vanessa's room. The door stood wide open: the bed was rumpled and a couple of IV bags hung from a rack, their ends pinched. "Oh, shit," he said, then went looking for the nurses' station and flagged one down.

"Yes, sir?"

"What's happened to Vanessa Baker, in 603?"

"She took a hike," the woman said.

"Is that a euphemism for died?"

"No, she was conscious, but on a gurney, with a private medical team surrounding her, plus her mother."

"Do you know what hospital they took her to?"

"The mother said she was taking her home."

"Do you have an address?"

The nurse checked her clipboard. "Which one? Mother or daughter?"

"Both."

"Oh, looks like they have the same address." It was an apartment building on Fifth Avenue, in the eighties.

Stone thanked her and slipped a hundred under the clip of the board. "Buy your girls a drink." He went back to where he had left Fred, got into the car, and gave him the address, then he called Bill Golding.

"Morning, Stone. Thanks for dinner last night."

"Are you divorced yet?"

"Not yet. I made it just in time."

"Tell me about Vanessa."

"Her mother checked her out of the hospital."

"I know, I was just there. How is Vanessa?"

"Conscious for short periods, utters a few words. Better than yesterday. I'm encouraged."

"Is taking her home going to help her or kill her?"

"I think she'll improve further at home, or I would have thrown myself across the bed and strapped her down. Her mother brought a doctor and two nurses. They were thoroughly briefed on her condition and progress before we allowed them to take her."

"Thanks, Bill."

"You're welcome."

Stone hung up as they pulled up to the awning on Fifth Avenue. He was immediately grilled by, first, a doorman, then a front-desk man. They called upstairs and he was allowed to take the elevator to her floor.

A uniformed maid answered the door. "Mr. Barrington?"

"Yes."

"This way, please."

He followed her across a comfortable living room and into a large bedroom next to it. French doors were open to a terrace, and Vanessa lay in a hospital bed where, presumably, her own bed usually was. A nurse, who was sitting beside the bed doing a crossword, stood up.

"Mr. Barrington?"

"Yes." Stone walked to the bedside and bent over Vanessa, who appeared to be asleep. Her eyes opened, and she managed a small smile.

"Hello, beautiful," Stone said. "You still with us?"

She puckered her lips, and he kissed them.

"Hey," she managed.

"She doesn't talk much, yet," the nurse said. "But she's getting better. You can have one minute, then she has to rest."

Stone pulled up a chair and took Vanessa's hand, which gave his a tiny squeeze. "Well," he said, "if you're going to talk my ear off, I'm leaving."

Her body gave a little twitch, which Stone interpreted as laughter.

"I'm going to come and see you every day," he said, "just to make sure you're getting better."

She smiled again.

"Time to go," the nurse said. "Don't wear her out."

Stone nodded, kissed Vanessa on the forehead, and left the room. Betty Baker was waiting in the living room, and she motioned him to a chair.

"How are you managing, Betty?"

"Better," she replied. "I'm satisfied that you didn't poison her, so I'm not mad at you anymore."

"I was told to be ready for the wrath of God."

"Mine is worse, but I no longer consider you a suspect."

Stone laughed. "For what it's worth, I've been told that someone slipped her the poison either during the dinner where we met or at the one the night before. Were you at the earlier one?"

"Yes. Quite a different crowd."

"Any Russians there?"

"None that I met. Of course, there was that Chekhov fellow at the Pierre."

"Right. I met him in Paris last week."

"Why?"

"Someone from home asked me to size him up."

"What were your conclusions?"

"All bad."

"We're agreed there," she said. "The man reeks of malevolence."

"How well put!"

"Was the person who asked you to size him up Lance Cabot?"

"Yes."

"I understand you have an association with him and/or his organization."

"I'm a sometime adviser. Sometimes I think Lance just wants someone to talk to who doesn't have an axe to grind, or want an ox gored."

"I've known him since he was a lad. His older brother and I had a little thing once, after we had both become single."

"He's taken an interest in Vanessa's misfortune," Stone said. "He has a lot of sources at his disposal, and I hope he'll be able to find out why this happened and who made it happen."

"I hope so, too."

"Has Lance called you?"

She shook her head. "I think he's still a little embarrassed by my, ah, association with his brother."

"Lance never forgets anything."

"I hope you'll come and see Vanessa every day," she said.

"I told her I would. I want to watch her getting better."

"So do I."

"Betty, may I ask you some questions?"

"Maybe," she said.

"Forgive me, but I was once a police officer, and some habits have stuck with me. When you learned about this, did anyone leap to mind who might have had reason to cause it?"

"Only you," she said, "and you only because you were the last person to see her . . . as she was. As I said, I got over that."

"Did you know Peter Grant before you and I met?"

"I knew him when he was in high school. His parents and I knew one another. I can't say I knew him well: he was just around, and he seemed like a very nice boy."

"Did you know that he had the acquaintance of Yevgeny Chekhov, the Russian?"

She shook her head. "I'd never heard of him until that evening."

"Do you know anyone who might wish Vanessa ill?"

Betty shook her head again. "No, she's not the sort to make enemies."

"There are always people who will misjudge others, and who hold grudges."

"I can't think of anyone like that in Vanessa's life."

"How about the business? Any toes get stepped on there?"

"Certainly not. She takes very good care of her people, and when we went public, she gave them stock."

"Good for her. Well, I'd better go." He rose.

"Thank you for coming, Stone."

"Think about my questions. If you remember anything pertinent, please call me." He gave her his card, then left.

eeing Vanessa alive and communicating had lifted a burden from Stone's shoulders, one he had not known was there. He had been afraid that he had somehow been an unwitting party to her poisoning. He went back to his office a different man from the one who had left there earlier.

"You're looking cheerful," Joan said, as she handed him his mail and messages.

"I'm glad you think so," he said. He had hardly sat down when Lance called, and they scrambled their phones.

"Bring me up to date," Lance said.

"I just saw Vanessa. Her mother moved her out of Bellevue and created a hospital room at home for her. She's cognizant of her surroundings and of the people around her, and she speaks a few words now and then."

"This is a big improvement over yesterday, then?"

"It is. Her doctors and, more important, her mother, are pleased. Betty, by the way, says that you and she are old acquaintances."

"Only in passing," Lance said.

"She gave the impression that she knew you better than that."

"I haven't seen her since I was eighteen," Lance said.

"Ah, that was a long time ago, wasn't it?"

Lance made a loud, throat-clearing noise that seemed to mean *shut up*, so Stone did.

"Have you heard from Holly?" Lance asked.

"Not for a while."

"I thought you might be seeing her while she's in New York."

Why hadn't she called? "I hope so."

"Give her my best," Lance said, then hung up.

Stone had started to look through his mail when the iPhone rang again, and he picked it up. "Hello?"

"Scramble," Holly said.

"Scrambled."

"I'm in town."

"So I heard. Thanks for the advance notice."

"I'm sorry, it was a last-minute decision. There was no time."

"Are you sleeping here?"

"I'd like that very much."

"Then your wish is granted. What time should I expect you?"

"Sixish?"

"Fine; alone or in company with others?"

"I'd love to see Dino and Viv."

"I'm sure they'd love that, too. We'll go someplace special."

"Where?"

"That will be a surprise."

"I'll look forward to it."

"Me, too." They hung up, and Stone called Dino.

"Bacchetti."

"Holly's in town. Viv here?"

"Yes, and we'd love to."

"The River Café at seven-thirty?"

"Done."

They hung up, and Stone buzzed Joan.

"Yes, sir?"

"Table for four at the River Café, seven-thirty."

"Yes, sir." She hung up, then buzzed him almost immediately. "Not until eight o'clock," she said.

"We'll have a drink at the bar, then. Bye."

Holly turned up at six sharp, but they didn't make it to the bedroom. The sofa in Stone's study did very well, with the door closed and locked to keep out curious staff.

When they were done, Holly sat on Stone's lap and sipped her drink. "Where are we dining?"

"I told you, it's a secret."

She wiggled a bit. "Tell me."

"You can go right on wiggling, but I shall not be moved, not even by something as much fun as that."

"Oh, all right. I have to get dressed now, and fix my hair, but I don't need to go upstairs for that."

Stone got dressed while she used the powder room mirror to restore herself.

In the garage at seven, Stone handed her a blindfold. "Put this on."

"You're overdoing the secrecy," she said.

"Nevertheless."

She put on the blindfold. "There."

"You know where, Fred," Stone said. "Take the scenic route."

Fred did his best to confuse Holly, and it worked until they got to a bridge.

"That noise is a bridge," she said.

"The Brooklyn Bridge."

"Then we're dining in Brooklyn?"

"Good guess."

They crossed the bridge and drove underneath it to the restaurant.

"Keep the blindfold on," Stone said. He got her out of the car and took her down to the floating terrace, then removed it for her.

"Glorious!" she said, looking across the East River at downtown New York City, its lights just coming on. "And my favorite restaurant!"

He took her inside where Dino and Viv were waiting at the bar. Everyone hugged and kissed.

The headwaiter approached. "Mr. Barrington, your table is ready."

They were seated by the big windows overlooking the river, then Holly waved at someone across the room.

"Who's that?" Stone asked.

"My old deputy secretary, now acting secretary, Maclean McIntosh. I didn't know they'd be here this weekend. I suspect they've come to visit his cousin, who has been under the weather."

"Anyone I know?"

"I don't think so. A woman named Vanessa Baker."

"I saw her this morning. She's recovering."

"From what?"

Stone brought her up to date on the poisoning.

"I'm glad I'm retired," Holly said, "or I'd have to be dealing with that in some way."

"Don't worry," Stone said, "Lance is dealing with it."

"I'm sure Mac will be relieved," Holly said.

"How are they related?" Stone asked.

"Their mothers are sisters."

"I saw her mother this morning, too."

"You do get around, don't you?" Holly said.

"I try." Stone looked up to see Peter Grant come into the restaurant with a woman. They were accompanied by another couple, the male of which was Yevgeny Chekhov.

"Ah," Holly said, "the odious Mr. Chekhov."

"Well put," Stone said, avoiding eye contact with them as they passed his table.

42

The group enjoyed themselves so much that they forgot about those around them. And when they left, Stone saw that Peter Grant's table and the McIntoshes had both left without him noticing. Fred was waiting for them, as was Dino's official SUV, and they were driven home.

The following morning, Stone and Holly, after making love and having breakfast, were watching MSNBC as a new poll among Democrats was announced. There were four other candidates, and Holly was leading all of them by at least ten points.

"How do you feel about the tracking polls?" Stone asked her.

"Like someone is looking over my shoulder. It amazes me that no one has discovered that I'm sleeping with you when I'm in New York."

"How have you managed that?"

"By taking a small room at the Carlyle and putting a staffer there. Also, they park my Secret Service SUV there. There's a little knot of press outside the hotel, waiting for me to come and go. All they see is an SUV with darkened windows drive in and out of the garage."

"That's clever."

"If I continue to improve in the polls, I'm going to have to start planning how to smuggle you in and out of the White House."

"It would be simpler just to continue the present arrangement, even after the election," Stone said.

"We'll get found out eventually," Holly replied. "Count on it."

Holly left the house in her SUV at mid-morning, and Stone had Fred drive him up to Fifth Avenue. Vanessa was sitting up in bed, looking alert. Stone kissed her and pulled up a chair.

"Better?" he asked.

"Better. I'm thinking more clearly." She said all this slowly.

"I saw your cousin Mac McIntosh in a restaurant last night."

"Yes," she said. "He was here"—she strugged a bit—"earlier."

"Want to try the *Times* crossword?" he asked. "I can read you the clues."

She nodded.

He read off a few of the easier clues, but she was having a hard time with it. "Maybe tomorrow," she said.

"Sure." Stone chatted on for a while, until she seemed to get sleepy, then he kissed her goodbye and left. He didn't see Betty in the apartment.

He walked over to Madison and found a table for lunch at La Goulue. The place was crowded and, as always, noisy, in the way of successful restaurants. He was about to order when Peter Grant suddenly filled his vision.

"Morning, Stone," he said. "I see you are alone. May I join you?"

"Of course, Peter."

"I just went by to visit Vanessa, but she was asleep and couldn't be disturbed."

"I was there earlier. She's making progress, but slowly."

"I hope that will improve," Peter said.

They both ordered salads, and Stone picked a wine. "Peter," he said. "Are you at all concerned about spending so much time with Yevgeny Chekhov?"

"Concerned? Why should I be?"

"He has a questionable reputation."

"That's overblown, Stone. People are suspicious of him because he's Russian and close to his president."

"Don't you think that's sufficient reason for suspicion?"

"That's just cold war hangover talk."

"He was KGB."

"A long time ago. Now he's just a businessman."

"What is his business?"

"He's an entrepreneur."

"Does his business involve him with removing his competition from competition?"

"That's not how they operate these days."

"There are a number of disappeared journalists and business competitors of his who, if they could speak, might tell you otherwise."

"Please don't be concerned, Stone. I know what I'm doing."

"Perhaps, but probably not as well as Chekhov knows what he's doing. He's the sort of fellow who could follow you into a revolving door and come out ahead of you."

"Ah, I believe that was said about Hungarians, not Russians."

"As a former NYPD cop, I can tell you that, among your guests the other evening, Chekhov is very likely the prime suspect in the poisoning of Vanessa Baker."

"That's preposterous," Peter said.

"Is it? Do you think Chekhov would hesitate to remove someone who got in his way?"

"I don't think he's that sort. And anyway, why would he have any ill feeling toward Vanessa?"

"Does he have any ill feeling toward you, Peter?"

"No, he doesn't. We're quite good friends."

"The police think she was poisoned at your dinner party, you know."

"No, I didn't know. Why do they think that?"

"The poison she was given is slow-acting; it takes twenty-four to seventy-two hours to have an effect. That puts your dinner party into the time frame."

"Do you think I had some part in this attack on Vanessa? We've been friends since childhood, and I love her dearly."

"No, I don't think that. Does Chekhov have any reason to be annoyed with you at the moment?"

"Certainly not. Why would you suggest such a thing?"

"Because you were sitting next to Vanessa when she could have been poisoned. Maybe she was not the intended victim."

Peter froze, his fork halfway to his mouth. It took him a moment to gather his thoughts. "Yevgeny and I are on very cordial terms. Neither of us has any ill feeling toward the other."

"I'm sure you know by now, Peter, that his class of Russian thinks about life very differently from you or I."

"He's never shown the slightest sign of any animosity toward me."

"The oligarchs operate very much like our American Mafia," Stone said. "They're very nice to people they're about to remove from the landscape."

Peter's hand trembled a bit as he put down his fork and beckoned a waiter for the bill.

"Lunch is on me, Peter. Think about what I've said. There may come a moment when you need some assistance. I'm here to help, if you'll let me."

"I don't think I shall need it, Stone. Now, if you'll excuse me, I have another appointment."

They shook hands.

"Don't wait too long to ask," Stone said. Peter turned and hurried from the restaurant.

43

tone called Lance, and they scrambled. Stone told him about his visit with Vanessa and his impromptu lunch with Peter Grant. He expressed his concerns for Peter.

"So, you think Peter could have been the poisoning target?"

"He was sitting next to Vanessa," Stone pointed out.

"So were you, Stone, on her other side."

"That's true."

"Did a waiter fill your water glass or pour you more wine?"

"I suppose so, but Chekhov has nothing against me."

"Of course he does," Lance said. "You've failed him."

"How so?"

"You have not continued to make money for him."

"That's pretty lame, Lance."

"Is it? Do you think Chekhov is incapable of murder with annoyance as his motive?"

"That would be insane."

"Granted, but it's still a motive. I think you would do well to avoid being in the same room with Chekhov, if not the same country."

"We were in the same room last night," Stone said, "and I'm still alive."

"The poison takes twenty-four to seventy-two hours to begin working."

"Oh, stop it."

"Peter and Mac McIntosh were there, too, I hear."

"Are you still having Peter followed?"

"Maybe. I don't like the idea of Mac and Chekhov being in the same room."

"Does Mac even know Chekhov?"

"He knows Peter Grant, that's enough."

"But you've just finished a major investigation that absolved Mac of any wrongdoing."

"Maybe we missed something. For instance, you thought Chekhov had left the country, but there he was at the River Café."

"That was certainly a coincidence."

"I agree, but perhaps his being there when Mac was present was not. Did you see them talk?"

"No, my back was to both of them. I didn't see them leave, either."

"Stone, the next time you have an opportunity for impromptu surveillance, surveil. All you had to do was change seats."

"Gotta run, Lance. Bye." Stone hung up.

Fred came into his office from the garage, both hands filled with shopping bags.

"Ah," Stone said. "I see Holly has looted Madison Avenue."

"Yes, sir. May I put them upstairs?"

"Yes, Fred, but take the elevator or you'll have a heart attack."

Fred left, and Holly was next in line. She flopped down in a chair next to his sofa.

"You look as though you could use a drink," Stone said.

"I could use a bottle of bourbon and a straw, to put it your way."

"One drink at a time," Stone said, and he poured her one from the liquor cabinet, then one for himself before joining her.

"How was your day?" she asked.

"I got a lot less done than you. Lance was on the phone: he was upset that Mac McIntosh and Yevgeny Chekhov were in the same room last night. Did you see them talking? You had a better view than I."

"No, they didn't speak or shake hands."

"Did you see them leave the restaurant?"

"The McIntoshes left shortly after we arrived. They must have booked for an earlier seating."

"Did you see Chekhov leave?"

"Five minutes before we did."

"All of which adds up to a big zero."

"What did you expect?"

"I had no expectations, but Lance did."

"Lance always expects the worst. It's an attribute of intelligence professionals. That way, if something terrible happens, they can say, 'I told you so.'"

Joan buzzed, and he picked up the phone on the coffee table. "A Peter Grant on one."

Stone picked up. "Hello, Peter."

"Stone, I'm sorry if I was rude in the restaurant today. I was very nervous, and I took it out on you."

"That's quite all right, Peter. What were you nervous about?"

"I'd rather tell you in person," Peter said.

"Then why don't you come over here for a drink about six?" Stone gave him the address, then hung up. "I offered him help, if he needed it. I guess he's going to take me up on the offer."

Holly looked at her watch. "I need a hot soak and a nap," she said. "What are we doing for dinner?"

"I booked us at Caravaggio at eight. You've got plenty of time."

Stone walked to the elevator with her, kissed her, then went to his study. He sat down with his drink and rested his head against the chair, then dozed.

He woke up at seven-twenty-five; Peter Grant had not shown up.

They got settled in at Caravaggio, which was already crowded, and ordered drinks.

"Did you meet with your friend?" Holly asked.

"He's not my friend, just an acquaintance, somebody I met socially in Paris."

"I had the impression you might be worried about him."

"I'm even more worried about him now. He didn't show."

"This is the younger man who was with Chekhov last night?"

"Yes. We had a quick lunch together today, and I told him that his association with Chekhov could put him at risk. He pooh-poohed the idea, but I told him to call me if he needed help."

"You mentioned that," Holly said.

"I'm sorry if I'm repeating myself."

"Is there anything you can do for him now?"

"I'll find out," Stone said, taking out his phone and looking at the recent calls list. He pressed the top one. It rang once, then went to a recorded message. Stone put his phone away. "His phone is no longer in service."

"Are you sure you got the number right?"

"It was the number he called me from this evening."

"And that was what, five?"

"Maybe a little later. I invited him over for a drink at six. Then, when you went upstairs, I went to the study with my drink and waited for him. Then I dozed off."

"What time did you wake up?"

"At seven-twenty-five."

"Do you have another number for him?"

"No, and I can't think of anybody who would."

"Then you've done all you can do," Holly said. "Relax, drink your drink, and concentrate on me." She squeezed his thigh under the table.

"That's easy enough," Stone said, turning toward her.

They finished their drinks, ordered dinner, and were halfway through that when Stone looked up to see Dino walking into the restaurant. He worked his way toward them, stopping to shake a hand here and there, then gave Holly a kiss, pulled over a chair from a neighboring table, and sat down.

"How'd you find me?" Stone asked.

"I tracked your cell phone, dummy. You think you can hide from me?"

Stone laughed. "I wasn't hiding, I'm just surprised."

"I wish I were the bearer of happy tidings," Dino said.

Stone put down his fork. "Tell me."

"About five-forty-five this evening, your pal Peter Grant lost control of his car on the West Side Highway, headed south, and turned it into a submarine. A brand-new Mercedes S-class, the souped-up one."

"Did he survive?"

"No. They got the car up about a half hour ago. The driver's-side window was blown out—or rather, had a fist-sized hole in it. He had taken a bullet in the head. A witness saw the car go in, but not the firing of the shot. There's always traffic on that road, and his car just peeled off the right lane, through an emergency parking area and a crash barrier and into the water. It sank quickly, I suppose because of the hole in the window, in twenty feet of water. A police tug and a diver were called and got it up."

"I've just got one question," Stone said. "Where was Yevgeny Chekhov when this happened?"

"Winging his way toward Paris in something called a Dassault Falcon 8. He took off from Teterboro about lunchtime."

"Peter would have been on his way to see me when he died," Stone said.

"Why?"

"I saw him at lunch, expressed my concerns about his relationship with Chekhov, and offered help, if he needed it. He called me around five—Holly was there when I got the call—and said he'd take me up on it. I invited him for a drink at six. He'd have been on time, if the traffic wasn't too bad."

"Do you want a look at the body?"

"No, thanks. I'd like to know what he had in his pockets, though."

"I'll find out," Dino replied. "Anything else I can do for you?"

"No. Thank you for coming, Dino. Do you have a next of kin on file?"

"No, we don't."

Stone took a card from his pocket. "Call Betty Baker at this number. She knows his family."

"Thanks." Dino pocketed the card.

"You got time for a drink?"

"Always," Dino replied. Their waiter seemed to have read his mind, or his lips, and arrived with a scotch.

"I want to learn that trick," Holly said.

"If you just think real hard about a drink, a waiter will get the message," Dino said.

The maître d' came over and looked at their plates. "Is anything wrong?" he asked.

"No," Stone said, "I'm just not hungry anymore."

"I am," Holly said, continuing to eat while Stone's plate was removed. "I want dessert, too. I didn't know the decedent."

Stone contented himself with his wine. "Excuse me for a minute." He took out his phone, called Lance Cabot, and scrambled. "Were your people still following Peter Grant?"

"They were three or four cars back and saw him take the dive. They called it in, then broke off. We still don't know what happened."

"I can help you with that. Dino just caught up with me and told me Peter was shot from another vehicle and took a bullet to the head."

"That's a bit less subtle than poisoning, isn't it?"

"Apparently, Chekhov was in a bit more of a hurry. By the way, he left for Paris around noon in a private jet. He was far from the scene when it happened, maybe even in Paris."

"I'd love to know what Peter knew," Lance said.

"He was on the way to my house when it happened," Stone replied. "I think he was going to tell me what you want to know."

Lance sighed. "That's the way it goes sometimes. They get worried too late."

"Exactly. I think maybe what happened to Vanessa Baker shook him. He realized that it could have been him—or maybe that it was intended to be him."

"I hope he kept a notebook," Lance said.

"Dino is going to examine the contents of his pockets. If he had something like that, we'll get it."

"Are you with Dino now?"

"Yes."

"Let me speak to him for a moment."

Stone handed the phone to Dino. "Lance wants to speak with you."

Dino took the phone, listened for a moment, then said, "Sure," and hung up. He handed the phone back to Stone. "He wants us to take the car apart, and Grant's clothes, too, to see if there's anything there."

"Good idea," Stone said.

"You want to see the car with me?"

Holly put down her fork. "Me, too. I'll have dessert later."

The police garage lights were on, so they got out of Dino's SUV. Peter's car was sitting in the middle of the ground floor, in plain view. Someone had left the driver's door open, so the shattered window could be seen.

A man wearing police coveralls came over to Dino. "Evening, Commish," he said. "What can I do you for?"

"Have you done anything with the Mercedes?" Dino asked, nodding toward the car.

"Not yet."

"Let's do it now. Take it apart and, when you're finished, put it on a lift."

"Yes, sir," the man said and waved to a pair of his colleagues. "Bring crowbars," he shouted.

"Can I have a look inside before you start?" Stone asked.

"Sure."

Stone went to the driver's door and looked around. Even though it had spent an hour or two in the Hudson River, it looked brand spanking new. The pedals had no wear on them and neither did the tires. He checked the center armrest compartment and found a current auto insurance certificate.

Dino opened the passenger door, then the glove compartment. "We got some paperwork here," he said.

He put on some latex gloves and handed Stone a pair, then removed an envelope from the glove box. "We got an equipment list here," he said, "and it's loaded. One hundred and fifty-six thousand dollars and change." He separated the list from the other papers and handed it to Stone. It was laminated in thin plastic, so was undamaged.

"Got a bill of sale and a title here," Dino said. "Damp. All cash, no trade-in, bought yesterday." Stone opened the rear doors and had a look back there, then he went to the trunk and beckoned to a man in coveralls. "Let's take everything out, down to the metal," he said, then stood back.

The man went to work, removing all the lining and an inflatable spare tire. Soon, all the bodywork was visible. Nothing to be seen. Stone went to the spare and turned it over. A thick, opaque, letter-sized zippered envelope was taped to the bottom of the tire.

Dino stepped up. "Whatcha got?"

"An envelope. Shall we open it?"

"Go ahead, don't mess anything up."

Stone pulled the envelope free from the tape, walked over to a desk on one side of the garage, unzipped it, and shook out the contents. Four passports and several stacks of cash—dollars and euros—fell out. Stone pushed the passports around with a gloved finger. One French, one Hungarian, one Polish, and one Maltese.

"Nice ready-kit," Dino said.

"Will you ask your guys to pull off the door panels and open the rocker panels, too?"

"Sure." Dino passed on the instructions. "How much cash do you reckon? A hundred grand of each currency is my guess."

"He could travel all over Europe with just one of those passports, then anywhere in the world he cared to go," Stone said.

"Commish, we've got more stuff in the doors." The man rooted out two more envelopes and put them on the desk.

Stone emptied them out. "More passports," he said. "Ireland and Iceland. More cash, too: Swiss francs. All the passports have photographs of Peter pasted in, but in different clothes and poses. In two of them, he's wearing a mustache or beard."

"You think he was getting ready to run?" Dino asked.

"Nope. Why would he spend a hundred and fifty-six grand on a new car? He couldn't drive it anywhere he could spend most of that money."

"No," Dino said, "I guess yesterday he was still feeling optimistic about life."

The men put the car on a hydraulic lift; the bottom was clean of any other evidence.

A car pulled into the garage, and Dave Pelly, the medical examiner, got out and walked over to the desk. "Here's what you asked for, Dino." He set a Macy's shopping bag on the desk and stepped back.

Dino emptied it onto the desk. "Small wallet," he said, picking it up. "Some debit cards and, here we go, a New York State driver's license."

"What address is on it?"

"It's 1010 Fifth Avenue," Dino said. "Same as on the bill of sale and title for the car."

"That's a co-op building," Stone said. "He must have bought something there."

"We don't need a warrant," Dino said. "He's the victim of a crime."

"Let's go, then," Stone said. The two of them and Holly got back into the SUV.

"Holly, do you want me to take you home first?"

"Not on your life. I'm fascinated."

They drove uptown.

The apartment was a spacious three-bedroom penthouse: LR, DR, library, and kitchen, overlooking the Metropolitan Museum of Art and Central Park.

"How much you reckon?" Dino asked Stone.

"I don't know: Six million, maybe?"

"That's what I figure, too."

On a table in the library, Stone found a legal-sized envelope and opened it. "Closing documents," he said. "Sale closed the day before yesterday. Six million five, all cash. He paid extra for the view."

The apartment contained a dozen or fifteen pieces of furniture, some of them with price tags still attached. There was a king-sized bed in the master with brand-new linens on it, unmade. They walked around some more.

The kitchen had a lot of stuff in Bloomingdale's shopping bags: everything you'd need to cook and eat. The living room contained a sofa, still wrapped in plastic, and a Steinway grand piano. Stone sat down and played a few chords. "Brand new," he said, "right off the showroom floor, eighty grand. No, he wasn't about to run."

It was midnight before Stone and Holly got back to his house, and they were both too tired to make love. They got into bed, naked.

"It's so sad," she said.

"What?"

"He went on a huge shopping spree and never got a chance to enjoy any of it."

"He certainly didn't enjoy his last ride in the car," Stone said.

"Does he have any family?" she asked.

"I don't know. Dino will find out tomorrow."

"I liked the apartment," she said. "I'd like to buy it."

"Holly, you can't go buying a six-and-a-half-million-dollar apartment while you're running for president."

"Well," she said, "there is that."

As soon as he got to his desk the next morning, Stone called Lance Cabot and scrambled, then brought him up to date on the searches of Peter Grant's car and apartment, including the passports and cash.

"That's a lot of passports," Lance said. "I'd like to see them."

"Call Dino. He can photograph them and e-mail them."

"No, I want the passports."

"Talk to Dino. They're not in my possession, nor will they be."

"I want you to do something for me," Lance said.

Stone sighed.

"Don't sigh. This is important."

"All right, Lance, what is it?"

"I want you to take Maclean McIntosh and his wife, Laura, to lunch today. There's a table already booked at the Grill. I was going to do it myself, but events have intervened."

"Is there something you want me to talk about?"

"Pump him for everything you can get on Peter Grant and Yevgeny Chekhov and their relationship, and I mean *everything.* And record it. You have a recorder? I can have one sent over."

"Please do that," Stone said. "I'm not sure I have anything adequate to the purpose."

"It will be there inside an hour, and call me when you're back home."

"All right. Anything else?"

"I want personal information on them, too."

"Surely you already have that."

"I want to see if there are any contradictions between what I know and what they tell you."

"How will I know?"

"I'll know. Transmit the recording to me. My man will show you how." Lance hung up.

Stone was waiting at Lance's table when the headwaiter brought the McIntoshes over. Stone switched on the recording device; the microphone was hidden in the silk pocket square in his jacket's breast pocket.

"Hello, Stone," Mac said, pumping his hand. "I didn't know you were joining us."

"Hi, Mac. Hi, Laura. I didn't, either, until Lance called. He's got some sort of flap going on at Langley and couldn't make the chopper to New York."

They got settled in at the table. "I think we should take the opportunity to explore the wine list, don't you?"

They both nodded happily.

Stone opened the wine list. "Shall we start with champagne?" He ordered a bottle of Dom Pérignon. "We haven't seen much of each other, so I welcome the opportunity to get to know both of you better." The champagne was served, and they studied the menus. They ordered, then Stone bored in. "You've heard about Peter Grant?"

"What about Peter?" Mac asked.

"He was driving on the West Side Highway around five-forty-five yesterday afternoon, when his car went into the Hudson."

Mac looked shaken. "Was he hurt badly?"

"He was shot in the head from another car. He's dead."

"I'm shocked," Mac said. Laura said nothing.

"How did you first meet Peter, Mac?"

"It was on Martha's Vineyard three or four years ago," Mac said.

"Three," Laura added. "We were staying with friends, and Peter was a houseguest, too."

"Who were your hosts?" Stone asked.

"Dan and Martha Thelwell," Mac answered. "We were at Harvard with Dan."

"Reason I ask is, the police don't have a next of kin to call, or even a cousin or a friend."

"He's from Boston," Mac said. "That's all I know. I didn't know him at Harvard."

"Where do the Thelwells live?"

"They've moved to London for Dan's work," Laura said. "We don't have an address."

"Who does he work for?"

"It used to be a Wall Street firm, but he got the London offer from another company, I don't know who."

"It's very sad," Stone said. "Peter had just bought an apartment on Fifth Avenue and a new Mercedes, which he was driving. I'm sure there'll be an estate to distribute, so if you speak to anyone who knows a relative, please let me know."

"Sure, but I don't expect we'll learn about that," Mac said.

"How well would you say you knew Peter?"

"Superficially," Mac said. "We only met him a couple of times after the Vineyard, always at some social event."

Stone changed the subject. "How did you two meet?" he asked.

"We had a class together at Harvard," Laura said.

"A class in what?" Stone asked.

"Russian history and literature, as I recall," Mac said.

"No," Laura broke in, "just history."

"She's always right," Mac said to Stone. "We also had some language classes in Russian together."

"Where were you both in school before Harvard?"

"I was at Phillips Exeter, and Laura was in the Spence School, here."

Their appetizers arrived, and Stone continued to question them while they started on their food.

"You know," Mac said. "Lance already has all this stuff."

"Oh, I'm not asking for Lance," Stone said. "I'm just interested. Do you mind?"

"Not in the least," Mac said.

"Tell me, after Harvard, how did you avoid the CIA? I'm sure they looked at you, especially if you had the Russian language."

"Not formally, but our Russian professor introduced us to a gentleman who asked us the sort of questions you're asking now," Mac said. "But, of course, you're now Agency, aren't you?"

"Only on the fringes," Stone said. "Once in a while I help out."

"As with our lunch today?"

"Exactly. I haven't done any personal shopping for Lance—yet—but I'm sure I'll get that call one day soon."

Stone got them through their decision to go to Washington, Mac in State, Laura at Defense.

"Has having Russian helped either of you in your jobs?" Stone asked.

"I was once asked to translate a telegram from Gorbachev to somebody, I forget who," Laura said.

"Me, never at all," Mac said. "I'm sure we're both pretty rusty by now."

"I wouldn't be surprised if Kate gave you the secretary's slot, now that Holly has resigned."

"Oh, that won't happen," Mac said. "There's no point in going through the confirmation process, when we'll have a new president in January. And Holly, if I know her, is going to want a woman in the job."

"Will you stay on at State?"

"That depends on who gets the top job," Mac said. "She may want her own deputy."

"What would you like to do if you leave State?"

"Write my memoirs," Mac said, laughing. "Seriously, I've got a book or two in me."

"I'll stay at Defense as long as they'll let me," Laura said.

Stone ordered an expensive bottle of claret, then their main courses arrived.

"Have you two traveled a lot?" Stone asked.

"I've accompanied Holly on a few official trips, but that's not traveling in the ordinary sense of the word. It's just hard labor."

"We like Italy," Laura said. "We have a little house in Tuscany that came to us from my side of the family."

"Have you traveled much in Eastern Europe?" Stone asked.

"We've been to Budapest a couple of times, and to Prague once."

"Ever put your Russian to use on the ground there?"

"Once," Laura said. "We both did a month in Leningrad as part of our studies when we were at Harvard."

"How did your language skills work?"

"After a week, pretty well," Laura said. "It was a valuable experience."

When they were on coffee, Mac said, "You know, our conversation sounds a lot like an employment interview for the Agency."

Stone smiled. "I thought I was craftier than that. Is that something that interests you? I could have a word with Lance."

The two of them exchanged a glance. "What an interesting idea," Mac said. "That had never occurred to me. What do you think, babe?"

"Rather a good idea," she replied, "as long as we don't have to split up. If we could retire, then we could take our pensions and what with two salaries from the Agency, we could live rather well."

"I'm not sure we'd have time to live well," Mac said. Then someone they knew stopped at the table to say hello, and the conversation ended.

S tone's phone was ringing as he walked into his office. He answered and scrambled.

"So?" Lance said.

"Joan is transmitting our conversation right now. I asked them how they knew Peter Grant—they professed not to know about his death. Both looked genuinely shocked. That's all on the tape, too."

"I'll call you back when I've listened to it." Lance hung up.

Lance called back more than an hour later. "Couple of interesting things," he said. "First, they didn't mention their month in Leningrad on their original employment applications at State and Defense. Second, the Thelwells from the Vineyard don't exist, just like Peter didn't, not in New York, Boston, or London. And no one by that name has ever worked at a Wall Street firm that has a London branch. Also, no one by that name has owned or rented a house on the Vineyard since the 1920s. However, during the time we're talking about, the McIntoshes were at an inn in Edgartown for two weeks, and Peter Grant was in the same hotel, along with an unidentified woman."

"That certainly is interesting."

"The failure to mention Leningrad could just have been an oversight, but when you put it together with the nonexistent Thelwells and Peter Grant, it makes more sense."

"What's your scenario?" Stone asked.

"A month in Leningrad studying Russian is a perfect opportunity for recruitment, if the process hadn't already begun at Harvard, and the later visit to the Vineyard put them in touch with Peter, who may have activated them at that time."

"You're assuming that Peter was an agent."

"I have always assumed that," Lance said. "Now I'm assuming that the McIntoshes are as well. I believe Mac is our mole at State. God knows what Laura has been reporting from the Pentagon."

"You heard me on the recording ask if they might be interested in joining the Agency."

"That was an inspired question, Stone. They'll report back to their handler on that. My guess is I'll get a call from Mac before long."

"They both appeared shaken by the news of Peter's death."

"They should be shaken," Lance said. "They're wondering if that could happen to them."

"Have you made any progress on a next of kin for Peter?"

"No, we're leaving that to Dino for the moment. It's his jurisdiction, and it's cheaper that way, too. Why don't you give him a call and find out what he's learned? I'd be very interested if the next of kin is also acquainted with the McIntoshes."

"I'll do that now," Stone said, then hung up.

———

"Bacchetti."

"It's Stone. I just got off the phone with Lance, and he tells me you're handling the search for Peter's next of kin. Found anyone?"

"No, because there isn't anyone. However, we went through that envelope we found in the apartment—the one with the closing documents—and it seems you discarded it a little too quickly."

"How so?"

"Peter executed a will at that closing, and the witnesses were those present. His lawyer notarized it."

"Who are his heirs?"

"There are four: Betty and Vanessa Baker get a quarter each, and the other half goes to a couple named Maclean and Laura McIntosh. Plus, his new apartment and its furnishings and the car go to Vanessa. He left a list of assets and account numbers and, essentially, the estate consists of his apartment and car and eighteen million dollars in cash and negotiable securities, after estate taxes."

"That," Stone said, "is more interesting than I can explain right now. I have to be somewhere." He hung up and asked Joan to summon Fred and the car.

He arrived at 1010 Fifth Avenue a half hour later and was admitted by the doorman and front-desk clerk, who knew him by this time. Upstairs, the door was opened by Vanessa's nurse who was, Stone thought, not very happy to see him.

He was led into the living room, where Vanessa, fully dressed and coiffed, was seated at the window in a wheelchair, with a notepad in her lap and a pencil in her hand. He kissed her and pulled up a chair, so she wouldn't have to make an effort to speak too loudly.

"You look absolutely lovely," Stone said.

"Thank you," she said slowly. "This is my first day of feeling lovely." She looked over her shoulder, where the nurse was standing. "Thank you, that will be all."

"But I . . ." the woman stammered.

"Please go," Vanessa said with emphasis, which appeared to cost her some strength. The woman went into the bedroom.

"Vanessa . . ." Stone began.

She held up a hand, then laboriously wrote something in block capitals on the steno pad in her lap, then showed it to Stone. BE CAREFUL WHAT YOU SAY, he read.

He nodded. "As you wish."

She erased the words. "Now," she said, "listen." She took a couple of deep breaths and said, slowly and barely above a whisper, "I know about Peter and the will. His lawyer called."

"Good," Stone said. "Does your mother know?"

"No, and I won't tell her."

"Then neither will I," he replied.

"Good." She stopped talking and just breathed for a moment.

He took the pad from her and wrote: *Is there anything I can do for you?*

She took it back and wrote: *Call Peter's lawyer, Bryce Gelbman, at Pierce & Gelbman. And tell him I want possession of the apartment and half the cash as soon as possible. Find me a nurse I can trust. Keep Mother out of this.*

Stone handed her his card. "Call me on my cell if you need me; I'll come right away."

She nodded and squeezed his hand. "Thank you for coming to see me, Stone," she said. "Goodbye."

He bent to kiss her on the cheek. "Do you feel safe here?"

"For the time being," she said. "We'll see."

Stone left the apartment and went home.

olly was home when he got there, and packing. "I'm off to-morrow morning," she said. "Can Fred drive me to the airport?"

"Of course, he'll be delighted. When you're done packing, come down to the study and have a drink. I've got some things to tell you."

"Give me a few minutes," she said.

Stone went downstairs and called Lance, making his report on Peter's estate.

"That rather confirms my suspicions about the McIntoshes," Lance said. "Was there anything on next of kin?"

"No. I would be interested to know who the extra woman was at the Vineyard inn, though."

"It's beginning to sound like Vanessa," Lance said.

Stone didn't want it to be Vanessa. "Is there any other evidence to back that up? Did they sign a register at the inn, or were reservations made in another name?"

"No, but it was noted that the extra woman had her own room. Were Peter and Vanessa ever romantically involved?"

"I doubt it," Stone said, "from the way she talks about him."

"How's she doing?"

"She's in a wheelchair now, and talking more. She wants to move into Peter's apartment as soon as possible. That reminds me, I've got to call Peter's attorney about that. Anything else?"

"Not for the moment."

Stone hung up, called Bryce Gelbman, and introduced himself. "Vanessa Baker wants to move into the new apartment as soon as possible," he said. "Is there a problem with that?"

"Not really. Peter put everything into a trust to avoid probate, and I'm his executor. So sure, tell her to go ahead. I left a key for her."

"Will you call her about that, please? Another thing," Stone said, "he also left her his car, and that's going to need some serious work after its swim in the Hudson. I think I can make a few calls and get the police to release it to you."

"Fine, I'll give it to the dealer and have them go to work on it."

"Bryce, have you learned anything about Peter's next of kin?"

"Apparently there isn't one. His parents are both dead. That's why he made a will and set up the trust."

"Is 1010 a co-op building?"

"Yes."

"How long did it take you to close it?"

"He bought the place shortly after his return to this country. Someone he knew is chairman of the co-op board, so he got through that step quickly. We closed as soon as he got board approval."

"Who did he use as references on his application?"

"I don't know; I never saw it. The Realtor handled all that." He gave Stone her name. "But, she said at closing that she was leaving the country the next day for a few weeks. I think she was spending her commission."

"Any idea where she went?"

"None at all."

"Thank you, Bryce. Let me know about the car." Stone hung up, and Holly walked into the room. He poured them drinks, and they sat down.

"So, what do you have to tell me?" she asked.

"I've been talking to Lance a lot, and he's convinced that the mole at State is Mac McIntosh."

She looked shocked. "But he was cleared in the investigation."

"I'm afraid they missed something."

"Apparently so did I," she said. "I don't know what to say to the press."

"You're going to say 'No comment, for reasons of national security.'"

"I hate to hide behind that."

"You're not hiding, it's a fact."

She sighed. "Oh, well. When is he going to be arrested?"

"Not immediately," Stone said. "Lance doesn't have his ducks in a row just yet."

"Good, because I don't want to deal with it yet."

"I don't blame you."

"May we have dinner here tonight? I don't feel like going out."

"Of course." He called Helene and gave her instructions, then his cell rang and he picked it up.

"Hello?"

"It's Vanessa," she said. "I can only talk for a moment, but I need your help on a couple of things."

"What can I do?"

"First, I need some discreet movers to pack a few things, move me into the new apartment, unpack, and arrange the things that are there."

"What else?"

"I need a new nurse. I don't trust the woman who's here now."

"Round the clock?"

"Yes, please."

"What time do you want the movers?"

"Around ten. Same with the nurses. Mother will be out of the house all day."

"Right. I'll call when it's all arranged."

"Don't call, text me. Mother will be home soon, and I don't want her to know where I am."

"As you wish." They said goodbye and hung up. Stone buzzed Joan and put her to work on Vanessa's requests.

"There," Stone said. "Now I can enjoy my drink."

A half hour later, Joan buzzed. "Vanessa is all set," she said. "The movers will be there at ten with four men, and the Carlsson Clinic is supplying the nurses. They'll be there at ten, too."

"Wonderful; please text Vanessa with the news." He gave her the number and hung up. "Where was I?" he asked.

"Drinking," Holly replied, "and I think we're both ready for another."

Shortly, Stone got a text from Vanessa: All is well, it read. Thanks.

————

They had just sat down to dinner when Lance called and scrambled.

"What's up?" Stone asked.

"I had somebody go to the Vineyard inn and talk to the proprietor. She remembered the name of the woman accompanying Peter: it's Baker. Something else. Peter's mother was the younger sister of Vanessa's mother, so she and Peter are first cousins. We're doing a full background check on her."

"I'm sorry to hear it."

"I want to wire Peter's apartment before Vanessa moves in."

"She's planning to move at ten tomorrow," Stone said. He gave Lance the apartment number, and Lance hung up.

"Why do you look so sad?" Holly asked.

"I've heard something I didn't want to hear," Stone said.

49

The following morning, Vanessa got up and slowly dressed herself, then the nurse served her breakfast. It was the maid's day off, and she waited for her mother to leave for the office before she summoned the woman.

"Miss Barlow," she said to the nurse.

"Yes, ma'am?"

"I'm feeling well today, and I want you to take the day off."

"I'm not sure you're up to that," she replied.

"I think I am, and it's time to find out. Mother will be back at noon. If I need anything, she'll get it for me."

The nurse brightened at the idea of the day off. "Well, if you're sure?"

"I'm sure."

"Then I'll see you tomorrow, Miss Vanessa." She got her handbag and left.

Vanessa walked into her bedroom and packed a small suitcase, then got back into her wheelchair. The movers and the first nurse arrived on time.

She led them around the apartment, pointing out which things she wanted packed and which should just be moved to the new apartment. She supervised them while they worked. She then felt rested enough to go downstairs and spread some hundred-dollar bills among the staff not to tell her mother where she was moving. "Your story is, the movers showed up and took my belongings away. I didn't leave a forwarding address. I will be using the name Carolyn Baum. Only those people using that name should be admitted to my floor or put through on the house phone." She went upstairs, unlocked her new apartment door, then went to the old one, got back into her wheelchair, and watched the movers remove everything. Satisfied that nothing was left, she wrote a letter to her mother, explaining that she was moving because she needed to handle the remainder of her recovery on her own. She left her keys on the hall table and went upstairs four floors, to the penthouse.

She supervised the unpacking and placing of her belongings, then sent the nurse out for groceries. She was done by three o'clock, then she called Stone.

"Hello?"

"Hi, it's Vanessa."

"How did the move go?"

"It's done; everything is unpacked and in its place. I've bribed the building's staff to tell my mother that I moved out without leaving an address, and I've sent out for groceries. For the time being, my name is Carolyn Baum. So if you visit, ask for that name."

"Is there anything further I can do for you?"

"Well, I'm going to need a car soon."

"Peter's car is being repaired and cleaned and should be ready in a few days, if you want to arrange a parking space for it. Bryce Gelbman is dealing with the insurance company on behalf of the estate, then he'll have it reregistered in your name."

"Wonderful. I'm not on any medication now, so all I need is time to get well. I'll call you when I'm ready to go out. In the meantime, if Mother calls, you know nothing. Tell her the staff told you I had moved out of the building."

"All right. If you need to run, come here, and I'll make you comfortable."

"Stone, do you think you can get me a new iPhone with a new number?"

"Certainly. I'll have it sent over to Ms. Baum in the morning."

"Thank you so much." She hung up.

It occurred to Stone that he and Bryce Gelbman were the only people outside her building who knew where she was. He asked Joan to arrange for the new phone, then, late in the afternoon he went to visit Vanessa Baker. Her mother answered the door.

"Good afternoon, Betty," he said. "I hope Vanessa feels well enough to see me."

She stared at him for a moment. "Come in, Stone."

Stone followed her into the living room and took a seat. "Is she feeling better?"

"I assume so," Betty answered. "She's moved out of this building without leaving a forwarding address."

Stone tried to look surprised. "Well, I'm sure she'll call you soon."

"Stone, look at me," Betty said, staring at him. "Where is Vanessa?"

"Betty, you just told me she has moved out."

"I know you know where she is."

"If I knew that, I'd have gone to her new address instead of here."

"She must have told *someone*," Betty said.

"Perhaps she's concerned, after Peter's death, that she might be in some danger."

"Why would she be in danger?"

"She was sitting next to Peter when she was poisoned. It's reasonable for her to think that it may have been intended for Peter. And then, of course, he was murdered."

She nodded. "Of course. I expect you're right. She'll be in touch."

Stone rose and excused himself, then went down to the lobby, to the front desk. "Would you ring Ms. Carolyn Baum and ask her if she'd like to see me?" he asked the desk man. "If she's indisposed, I can come back."

The man rang the apartment and hung up. "You may go right up, Mr. Barrington. She's in the penthouse."

Stone rode the elevator up and rang the bell. Vanessa came to the door under her own steam. "Come in, Stone."

Stone went in and took a seat on the sofa, the only piece of furniture in the room except for the piano. "This is going to be very nice," he said.

"Yes, it is. A friend of mine, a stage designer, is coming over tomorrow to talk about what to fill it up with. She has a lot of contacts for renting or buying furniture. Would you like a drink? Peter stocked the bar."

"Thank you, yes, but I'll get it."

She pointed to the cabinet. "It's behind the bookcase, just pull."

Stone pulled the bookcase, revealing a full bar behind it. "Would you like something?"

"I think it's too soon for me to drink."

Stone came and sat down again. "I saw Betty a few minutes ago."

She looked alarmed. "Why?"

"I thought it might seem odd if I stopped coming to see you. She grilled me thoroughly, but I told her nothing. May I ask why you don't want her to know where you are?"

"I suppose you have a right to ask," Vanessa said. "I'm not sure I can trust her."

Stone took a breath, then asked why.

"Please don't ask," she said. "Just keep my secret for the time being."

"All right," Stone said, "I will."

50

The following morning, Stone and Holly had breakfast and goodbye sex, then she left for the airport. Stone went down to his office, called Lance Cabot, and scrambled. "Vanessa Baker has moved out of her mother's apartment, into Peter Grant's place in the same building. Peter had left her the apartment, the car, and a quarter of his cash."

"Interesting," Lance said.

"I went to see her in the old apartment, pretending I knew nothing, and spoke to her mother, Betty, who seemed angry that Vanessa had left."

"Perhaps she was just feeling motherly," Lance said.

"There was nothing motherly in her attitude," Stone replied. "Also, I mentioned that Peter had been murdered, and she didn't bat an eye. She wouldn't have known he was murdered. The police have never released that."

"Now that's downright ominous," Lance said. "Do you think she had a hand in it?"

"I think Vanessa thinks so. She went to some lengths to make her mother believe that she had moved out of the building, bribing the staff and hiring new nurses."

"Can she get away with that?"

"I don't see why not," Stone replied.

"How far was Betty sitting from Vanessa at the dinner you attended?"

"Betty was seated on my left, Vanessa on my right."

"Did she move around and speak to other guests?"

"She did some of that before taking her seat. I remember she greeted Peter with particular warmth, and he was sitting on Vanessa's other side."

"Perhaps Betty has chosen sides, and not Vanessa's."

"Have you heard anything more about Yevgeny Chekhov?"

"He's back at the Russian embassy in Paris," Lance replied. "Apparently, he keeps an apartment there."

"How long has he had it?"

"I don't know. It didn't come up until you lunched there with him and Peter."

"Do you have people on him in Paris?"

"From time to time," Lance said. "We're informed when Chekhov leaves the embassy."

"Has he left much?"

"No, but yesterday he had half a dozen visitors. They all arrived in Bentleys and Rollses."

"Sounds like a board meeting," Stone said.

"Of what company?"

"You tell me," Stone said.

"I wish I could. Do you have any idea where his apartment is located in the embassy?"

Stone thought about that. "When I entered the building from the front door, I was taken down a fairly long corridor past the ambassador's office and, perhaps some others, then into a circular courtyard. When Chekhov and Peter appeared, they came from the rear of the building into the courtyard, at perhaps a hundred-and-eighty-degree angle from the ambassador's office. Perhaps there are quarters there for the ambassador, some embassy officers, and a guest: Chekhov."

"I'll pass that along and see what my people can make of it. Keep me abreast of Vanessa and her activities." Lance hung up.

Stone called Dino.

"Bacchetti."

"It's Stone. Peter Grant's executor has asked that Peter's Mercedes be released to the estate. Do you have any reason to hang on to it?"

"I'll call the ADA on the case. I think we've got whatever it had to give us."

"Thanks. Vanessa is going to need a car." He explained to Dino about her moving.

"There's a girl who wants to get away from her mother," Dino observed.

"Right. Holly left this morning. How about lunch?"

"Let's go to La Goulue and look at the girls."

"I take it Viv is traveling."

"How'd you guess? One o'clock?"

"Right." They both hung up and Stone asked Joan to make the reservation.

Before lunch, Stone made the trip uptown and was admitted to Vanessa's apartment. She had very good privacy, since the apartment took up the whole floor. Vanessa wasn't using the wheelchair; they had a drink on the terrace, overlooking the Metropolitan Museum.

Vanessa wasn't very talkative, and Stone didn't know if she was having difficulty with speech or just preferring quiet.

"Vanessa," he said, trying to draw her out, "do you remember going to Martha's Vineyard with Peter three or four years ago?"

She looked at him. "No."

"I believe you stayed at an inn in Edgartown; the McIntoshes were there."

"Peter and I didn't sleep together, ever."

"You would have had a separate room."

She shook her head. "No, I don't remember such an occasion."

"Have you had trouble with your memory since you were poisoned?"

"With my speech, yes; with my memory, no. I would certainly have remembered that visit, if I had been there, but I don't suppose I've been to the Vineyard for five or six years. Why would you ask about such a meeting?"

"Never mind, it's nothing."

"Have you heard anything more from my mother?"

"No. After our conversation yesterday, she would have thought that, if I knew where you were, I would have told her."

"I suppose so."

"Vanessa, what do you suppose your mother would do if she learned where you are?"

"I have no way of knowing that," Vanessa said. "I just want to avoid seeing her, if I can. And I'm just as safe a few floors up as I would be in another building across town."

"Are you concerned about your safety?"

"Wouldn't you be, if you had just been poisoned?"

"I suppose I would be, but I'm glad you feel safe here."

"'Safe' is a relative term. I'm not sure I'll ever feel safe again."

"Have you had any further ideas about who might have done this to you?"

"No, none."

"Do you think your mother is involved?"

"I can think of no reason why she might want me dead. We've always had a good relationship—like sisters, really."

"But now?"

Vanessa looked out at Central Park for a moment, then back at Stone. "I'm afraid of her," she said.

Dino tore a roll in two and stuffed his mouth. "She's afraid of her mother? Didn't they live together?"

"Not anymore." Stone explained the situation.

"Is her mother a drunk or an addict?"

"No evidence of that. She has a drink when I'm there."

"Well," Dino said. "If Vanessa is afraid of her mother, then I'm afraid *for* Vanessa."

"So am I, but I don't know what to do about it."

"Get her out of there."

"She's just moved in, and she likes it."

"How's her recovery coming?"

"She's been in a wheelchair, but not the last time. She seems pretty normal."

"Does she want sex?"

"No sign of that."

"When she wants sex, that's when she's normal. Then get her out. You've got plenty of room, and Holly has split."

"I've offered, but she hasn't taken me up on it."

"Does the mother know about Peter's will?"

"I don't think so. If she did, she'd know about the apartment."

"Sooner or later the mother is going to get a letter from the executor, and she'll know about the apartment; you'd better get Vanessa out before that happens."

"I'll see what I can do," Stone said.

After lunch, Stone went back to Vanessa's. She greeted him at the door with a warm, lingering kiss. "I think I must be all well," she said.

Stone followed her into the bedroom. The nurse was nowhere in sight.

"The nurse is shopping," Vanessa said, unzipping her dress and letting it fall to the floor. She was naked. "I gave her a long list," she said, working on Stone's buttons.

A half hour later they lay in each other's arms, panting. "How do you feel?" Stone asked.

"Better than I have since the fateful dinner," she replied.

"Then you're going to need regular attention," he said, "and that's best done at my house."

"I like it here."

"Shortly, Betty is going to get a letter from Bryce Gelbman, informing her of the existence and contents of Peter's will. Then she will be looking for you here."

"I hadn't thought of that," she said.

"Pack a couple of bags. Fred is downstairs with the car. We'll make you very comfortable at my house."

Vanessa got to her feet, and Stone watched her closely, to see if she had any balance problems. There were none. The nurse returned and was dismissed.

Stone installed Vanessa in the master bedroom and helped her put her clothes in the dressing room. "You take a nap, then come down to the study at six, and we'll have a drink before dinner."

"I feel up to going out," Vanessa said.

"Betty knows too many people; we shouldn't be seen together right now."

"Oh, all right, I'll see you at six."

At six, Stone poured them both a drink and sat down beside her on the sofa. "I've had a thought," he said. "I've got houses in England and France—also L.A.—and I have an airplane. Paris is not a good idea right now, because Chekhov is there."

"So, it's England or L.A.? Are we safe in London?"

"I have a country place, as well. Betty is unlikely to turn up on the doorstep."

"Where is your house in L.A.?"

"At the Arrington Hotel. It's a separate house, very private."

"Let me think about it," she said.

Over dinner, Stone asked, "How long have you lived with Betty?"

"Not since I was eighteen," she replied. "She's lived with me for nearly six months while her apartment is being renovated."

"You own two apartments at 1010?"

"I do. When she moves back to her place, I'll sell the one downstairs."

"When is she scheduled to move back into her own place?"

"Three months ago," Vanessa replied. "Maybe I can hurry the process a little."

"How?"

She explained her plan.

The following morning, early, he phoned Betty.

"Hello, Stone," she said without enthusiasm.

"Good morning, Betty. I've heard from Vanessa."

"Where is she?"

"I don't know. We spoke on the phone, but she wouldn't tell me where she's moved. She asked me to speak to you and say that she's going to put the 1010 apartment on the market today, so you should expect a Realtor to turn up with prospects."

"That's very inconvenient," Betty said.

"Vanessa says that you have an apartment of your own, and it's silly to keep money tied up at 1010. Surely your apartment can be moved into after six months."

"There were delays."

"Then I'm afraid you'll have to live with that. She'd like you to move immediately. She wants the furnishings for her new apartment."

"I don't really feel like moving," Betty said.

"Then I'll have to have you removed."

"You can't do that!"

"Betty, you're a guest, not a tenant. You don't have a lease. All I have to do is to have your things put in storage and change the locks."

"Tell Vanessa I want to talk to her first."

"She says she doesn't want to speak with you, that everything she has to say was in her letter to you."

"This is very unkind of her."

"It was very kind of her to allow you to stay in her home for six months. The first prospective buyers will be there at one o'clock, and there will be others before the day is out. The Realtor has the key, and she'll let herself in. Please ask the housekeeper to tidy up after you. Goodbye, Betty." Stone hung up, and turned to Vanessa. "Why do you think this is going to work?"

"She won't be able to live with Realtors and viewers prowling around the place. She has a thing about her privacy. She'll go."

52

Stone arrived at 1010 Fifth Avenue late in the afternoon, and was allowed access by the front-desk man. "Is Mrs. Baker in?" he asked.

"No, sir," the man replied, "she moved out a lot of stuff this morning and said she wouldn't be back."

"Did she leave her key?"

"No, sir."

Stone went upstairs and used Vanessa's key to let himself in. "Hello?" he called.

"Hello?" a woman's voice said, then the maid came into the foyer. "Hello, Mr. Barrington," she said. "I wasn't expecting you."

"Is Betty here?"

"No, sir. She moved out this morning, said she was going back to her own place. I've been cleaning all day, getting the place ready to be shown."

"Please go on with your work," Stone said, then he called Vanessa's cell number.

"Hello?"

"I'm in. Are you upstairs?"

"Yes."

"You can come down now. The maid is here cleaning."

"I'll be right there." She hung up.

Stone took a look around the place: it seemed very clean and less cluttered with bric-a-brac.

Vanessa let herself in. "Brenda?" she called, and the maid came out of a bedroom and greeted her warmly. "You can go on cleaning," Vanessa said. "There won't be any buyers looking today. And, Brenda?"

"Yes, ma'am?"

"My visit here is just between us. I don't want Mother to know where I am or what I'm doing."

"I understand, Ms. Baker." She went back to work.

The house phone rang, and Vanessa picked it up. "Yes? Please send him right up." She hung up. "It's the locksmith."

"Tell him what you want done," Stone said. "I'll have a seat in the library."

He went into the room and found an interesting book.

An hour later, Vanessa came into the room and handed him some keys. "These are for you—both apartments; they're marked. Brenda will start working upstairs tomorrow and will dust in here each day. I've called my Realtor, and she'll be here in a few minutes. Her office is just around the corner. I'm expecting my decorator friend in an hour or so."

"I'm happy here," Stone said. "If there's anything you want to take to my house, we'll just put it in the trunk of the car."

Stone went back to his reading. After a few minutes, he heard the house phone ring, and after that, the doorbell. Vanessa came into the library with a middle-aged woman in a Chanel suit. "Stone, this is Margot Goodale, my Realtor. Margot, this is my friend Stone Barrington. He's also my attorney and can speak for me." They left the room.

Finally, Vanessa came back alone and made them both a drink. Margot says we'll ask six million nine and take six and a half."

"That's what Peter paid for the penthouse," Stone replied.

Vanessa sat down in a neighboring chair. "Somehow I feel I've crossed a river in my life," she said. "Mother is out of my hair, now, and I want to keep it that way."

"I'll do what I can to help," Stone said, "and I'm happy to have you stay on with me as long as you like."

"I'm going to take you up on that," Vanessa said. "I'd rather be there than in London or L.A. right now."

"Good. I take it from your earlier conversation that you want me to represent you?"

"I'd like that very much."

"I'm pretty much in the advice business these days," Stone said. "When you have a need for actual legal work, like selling this apartment, I have a small group of lawyers at Woodman & Weld who handle that sort of thing. It's run by another partner, Herbert Fisher; you'll meet him eventually. If I'm ever out of touch, call my secretary, Joan, and she'll connect you with Herb."

"Good to know."

The decorator arrived, and Vanessa introduced her as Jean Swift. "Stone is both my friend and my attorney," Vanessa said to her. "You can always speak freely with him."

"I'll keep that in mind," Jean said.

Vanessa excused herself for a moment.

"Something I think you should know, Stone," Jean said. "I've had a couple of calls from people looking for Vanessa—one a man, the other a woman, both with accents I couldn't place."

"Might they be Russians?"

"They might very well be."

"Did either of them leave a number?"

"The man did. It's one familiar to me, the Pierre Hotel."

"I know that one," Stone replied. "Don't tell Vanessa just yet. She needs a few days to get settled before we bother her with such news."

Vanessa came back and took Jean away, along with two large totes containing catalogs and photographs. Stone went back to his book. He could hear the two women moving about the apartment. He was dozing in his chair when they returned.

"All right," Jean said. "I have my list of what furniture and art you want moved upstairs, and I'll get that done tomorrow."

"Good," Vanessa said. "Hang the pictures as you see fit."

"And I'll place the orders for the things you chose from the catalogs."

"Wonderful." The two woman air-kissed and Jean left.

"Sit down, and let's talk for a moment," Stone said.

Vanessa sat.

"Jean told me she's had a couple of calls from people looking for you—a man and a woman. The man left the number of the Pierre and a suite number. He said his name was Smith, but I doubt that very much."

"What do you want me to do about them?"

"Ignore them. I gave Jean my number and asked her to refer any such calls to me."

"That's fine with me."

"She said that both people had foreign accents, and that they might be Russian."

"I don't like the sound of that," Vanessa said.

"Neither do I," Stone said. "Do you have any experience with firearms?"

"Yes, I had a boyfriend once who was a gun nut. He got me a carry license."

"Do you own a gun?"

"Yes, but I have no idea where it is."

"I'll give you something small and light to keep with you."

"Perfect," she said. "What do you think these calls mean?"

"I think they mean that Yevgeny Chekhov is looking for you," he said. "I wonder why."

Vanessa gave him a big shrug.

A t Stone's house again, Vanessa went upstairs for a nap, and
Stone called Lance Cabot and scrambled.

"We got Betty Baker out of Vanessa's old apartment, and
she's put it on the market."

"Any news on why Vanessa is afraid of Betty?"

"No. However, two people tried to reach Vanessa through her
decorator. They both had accents, maybe Russian, and one left the
phone number and a suite number that's at the Pierre Hotel."

"I believe that is Yevgeny Chekhov's preference in New York,"
Lance replied. "What, I wonder, does he want with Vanessa?"

"Perhaps he believes that Peter Grant shared information
with her."

"Information that he murdered Peter for."

"Lance, I questioned Vanessa about the meeting with the McIntoshes on the Vineyard. She denies having been to the island in the
past five years."

"What do you read into that?"

"I think, perhaps, that the Ms. Baker who was registered there was Betty." Stone waited half a minute or so for Lance to get around to responding.

"So, we had two suspected traitors, one presumed traitor, and one possible traitor, all in the same nest for a few days."

"Yes, we did."

"And these are all people who, like me, have known Betty since childhood."

"Yes."

"Then I conclude from that information that Betty Baker is the hen on the nest of this brood of spies."

"I think that's a not unreasonable conclusion," Stone said.

"I also conclude that Vanessa figured this out, and that is why she's afraid of her mother. Has she said or done anything that would make you think this?"

"Nothing, but I haven't pressed her on the subject."

"Perhaps it's time you did, Stone," Lance said. "You might save us a good deal of time and expense."

"I will do so when I think the time is right," Stone replied.

"Stone"—Lance sounded irritated—"I think you'd better accept my judgment on this."

"Lance," Stone said, feigning patience, "you haven't seen or spoken to any of these people for years, and one of them is dead. Are you receiving messages from the Beyond?"

Lance was silent.

"Then apart from your boyhood memories, I seem to be in a better position to make that judgment than you."

"Very well," Lance said at last.

"I'll call you when I have more to report. In the meantime, you could be very helpful if you assigned some of your flock to determine where the McIntoshes are and what they are doing there."

"I'll see what I can do," Lance said, then hung up.

Joan stuck her head inside the door. "Anything I can do, or is all this still none of my business?"

"For the time being," Stone said. "I'll trust you later."

Late in the day, Lance called and scrambled.

"Yes, Lance?"

"The McIntoshes, you'll be interested to know, are vacationing in Martha's Vineyard, in the same Edgartown inn as before. They have one guest, a Mrs. Baker."

"Thank you," Stone said. "Are you well-represented there?"

"We have a one-man station at present: a retired Agency officer named Percy Willard, elderly but spry. I have dispatched reinforcements."

"Good to know," Stone said, then hung up and buzzed Joan.

"Yes, sir?"

"Please call the yacht and have it moved to Edgartown, Martha's Vineyard, in the marina, if there's space. I'd like it there by mid-morning tomorrow. Faith is back from her training, isn't she?"

"Yesterday."

"Please tell her I'd like the airplane ready to taxi at ten AM, destination: the Vineyard. She should call ahead about parking space on the ramp, and she should bring another pilot, even though I'll be flying left seat."

"Will do," Joan said.

Stone hung up and called Dino.

"Bacchetti."

"It's Stone. Is Viv in town?"

"Arrived this afternoon."

"How would the two of you feel about a few days aboard *Breeze* on Martha's Vineyard?"

"I think I speak for us both when I say, Hell, yes!"

"We taxi at ten AM."

"See ya." Dino hung up.

He went to wake up Vanessa, in the nicest possible way.

She pulled his face into her lap, and shortly, she was wide awake. When they were both exhausted, he said, "How would you like a few days aboard a yacht?"

"I think I would like that very much. Where's the yacht, and whose is it?"

"It will be at the Vineyard tomorrow morning, and I'm one of its three owners. Dino and Viv will be coming with us."

"So, I'll need yachting clothes?"

"Of the more casual kind, and you can shop in Edgartown, if you like. You'll need one nice dress for dinner."

"I think I can manage those things. How long will we be gone?"

"A few days. I don't know how much time Dino and Viv have off."

"Has it occurred to you that tomorrow is the Fourth of July?" she asked.

"You're right. I had momentarily forgotten. Then they should at least have the long weekend off. We'll be lucky to get a marina berth, but that's okay. We can always anchor in the harbor."

She bit him lightly on a nipple and summoned him to duty once again.

"I believe you have entirely recovered," he said, making himself available to her.

"I believe I have," she replied.

They entertained each other until cocktail time, when they dressed and went down to the study.

Fred came in. "Dinner in fifteen minutes?" he asked.

"Perfect," Stone said, mixing them drinks.

54

The airplane was on the ramp with the airstairs door open and inviting. Faith and another woman, both in summer uniform, awaited them at the door, as a lineman unloaded their luggage and stowed it.

"I hadn't expected anything quite so big," Vanessa said as they climbed aboard. Dino and Viv were already seated in the cabin, drinking coffee.

Stone got Vanessa settled and poured her coffee, then excused himself and went forward to the cockpit. Faith awaited him in the right seat, and the second pilot was settled in a crew seat.

"We're at the point in the checklist where it says 'Start engines,'" she said, passing him the handbook.

Stone started the engines and, while Faith ran the rest of the checklist, looked at their clearance, already programmed into the flight computer and displayed on the pilot's and copilot's displays. Faith called ground control for taxi clearance, then Stone began to move the airplane. He was aware of some movement behind him so he turned and found Vanessa being buckled into the jump seat and given a headset.

"This I've got to see," she said.

Stone turned back to his work and taxied to runway one. There was no waiting, as the holidaymakers had mostly departed the previous day. He was cleared for takeoff, then lined up and moved the throttles forward. Shortly, he pulled back on the sidestick, and the airplane rose into the air. Faith was working the radios, like a good copilot, and soon traffic control gave them an altitude of fifteen thousand feet, direct to the Vineyard.

He leveled off at the assigned altitude and reduced power to cruise, then checked the screen before him. ETA was thirty-five minutes.

After leaving the New York air traffic center, he was handed off to Boston Center, then was given a descent to five thousand feet, and the island came into view in the distance. "Cancel IFR," Stone said. "I want a look at the harbor."

Faith made the call, canceled their clearance, and they were told to maintain the same squawk code. Stone descended to three thousand feet and slowed. "You watch for traffic," he said to Faith. He swung wide to his right and made a turn, keeping the harbor on his left wingtip. "There's *Breeze*," he said. "We got a berth."

He leveled the wings for a moment to get them headed offshore before turning for the airport, and he pointed to an area outside the harbor, where a very large yacht was anchored. "Look at her," he said. "She's got to be more than three hundred feet; she'd never fit in the marina and not even in the harbor on a crowded holiday weekend."

He turned left and descended to fifteen hundred feet. "Vineyard Airport, N123TF, six miles out, left base for two four. Anybody in the pattern?" He was greeted by silence.

"No visible traffic," Faith said.

Stone turned final for runway twenty-four and aimed at the numbers. The runway was only 5,500 feet, and he didn't want to use it all. He touched down, reversed the engines, and braked, then turned off the runway with two thousand feet to spare. He taxied to the ramp and shut down, while a tractor met him, ready to tow the Gulfstream 500 to parking elsewhere.

A big SUV drove up with his yacht's captain, Brett, at the wheel. Linemen stowed their luggage, and they were off for the Edgartown marina, chatting along the way.

"Did you get a look at the superyacht outside the harbor?" Captain Brett asked.

"A good look," Stone replied.

"Three hundred forty feet! Their captain somehow expected to be accommodated at the marina. I heard some conversation with the harbormaster on the radio about it. They were told to drop anchor outside, but they didn't like it."

"What's her name?" Stone asked.

"*Tsarina*. I got a look at her stern as they departed the harbor."

Stone found the name a little unsettling. His phone rang.

"Scramble," Lance said.

"Scrambled," Stone replied.

"Bad news," Lance said. "The party canceled their reservations at the inn."

"I think I know why," Stone replied, then told him about *Tsarina*.

"That sounds like what Chekhov would name a yacht," Lance said. "I'll see that we have some people waterborne."

They drove into the marina parking lot, where two crewmembers from *Breeze* awaited with luggage carts, and soon they were aboard.

Vanessa stopped as she entered the saloon. "Perfectly beautiful," she said.

"Come have a look at our cabin."

She followed him below and was suitably impressed by their quarters.

"Have a seat," Stone said. "I have something to tell you."

She did so. "Is this bad?"

"No, not at all. It's just information. Lance Cabot called me yesterday and told me that Mac and Laura McIntosh had reservations at an inn in Edgartown, along with a guest named Baker. It's the same inn where they brought Peter three years ago."

"Then they're here?"

"Not at the inn. Lance called to say they had canceled. But there's a huge yacht anchored outside the harbor called *Tsarina*."

"I think I'm getting the picture," Vanessa said. "It's Chekhov, isn't it?"

"That's my best guess. Who else would name his yacht after a dead Russian empress?"

"How can I avoid Mother?" she asked.

"Just stay aboard. We'll be dining here, anyway, but if you go shopping, you just might run into someone from their party. It's up to you how you want to handle that."

"Well, I had counted on buying some things here," she said. "Do you know when they arrived?"

"They may not even be here yet. I expect that when they are, they'll go directly to the yacht, just as we did."

Vanessa stood up. "Then I'd better go shopping now," she said, "before they start to roam."

Stone went to his bag and produced a small semiautomatic pistol. "Then take this with you, just in case. You know how to work it?"

Vanessa popped the magazine and ejected the round in the chamber onto the bed, then reloaded, pumped a round into the magazine, and set the safety. "I do," she said.

"I'll ask Viv to go along, too. She's always armed."

"Under what circumstances should I shoot somebody?"

"Only when it's absolutely the only way out of whatever predicament you're in," Stone replied. "And if you have to, try not to kill anybody. Of course, if they're shooting at you—or about to—go for the middle of the chest or the head, depending on how close they are."

Vanessa took a deep breath and exhaled. "Okay," she said, tossing the pistol into her handbag, "Let's go."

55

Vanessa and Viv got themselves together to leave the yacht, and Stone took Viv aside. "Did you see the huge yacht outside the harbor?" he asked.

"I did. Is it Chekhov's?"

"I expect so, and I expect the McIntoshes and Vanessa's mother, Betty, to be aboard her by dinnertime, perhaps sooner."

"I'll watch myself and Vanessa, too," she said, patting her waist where her pistol resided.

"Vanessa is packing, too, and she seems to know how to handle it."

"Good."

"Don't shoot each other," he said, then watched them walk down the boarding steps and off toward the center of Edgartown.

Dino stepped up beside him. "Are you thinking what I'm thinking?"

"Yes," Stone replied. "Let's go." He put on a light jacket to conceal his weapon, and they went up the dock and ashore, then looked around. "Do you see them?"

"No," Dino said. "How could they disappear so fast?"

"Into a shop," Stone said. "Let's have a seat." He pointed at a bench. The two settled there and had a clear view of downtown Edgartown.

Dino got fidgety. "Where the hell are they?"

"Have you forgotten how long it takes two women to shop?" Stone asked.

"Four times as long as one woman," Dino replied.

"They're in one of the shops we can see. They didn't have time to get any farther."

A tall, elderly man, clad in white trousers, deck shoes, a blue sailing jacket, and a rumpled tennis hat blocked their view. "Shove over," he ordered.

Stone and Dino moved over, and he sat down.

"I believe we have a mutual acquaintance, Mr. Barrington."

"Oh?"

"I'm Percy Willard," he said, not offering a hand. "Your women are in the shoe shop over there." He nodded rather than pointed.

"Oh, God," Dino said, "not the shoe shop! They'll be in there all day."

"You would know better than I," Percy said. "My wife's been dead for fifteen years."

"I hear you're station chief here, Percy," Stone said.

"Not much of a station," he replied. "Just me. And call me Perce."

"I'm Stone, he's Dino."

They sat silently and waited, while Perce pretended to read a *New York Times*.

"Will you join us for dinner aboard *Breeze*?" Stone asked.

"I'm a Connecticut Yankee," Perce replied, "and as such, I never turn down anything free. What time?"

"Come at six-thirty for free booze."

"How dressed?"

"Up."

"May I bring a date?"

"Of course."

"You talked me into it. You've seen *Tsarina*?"

"Hard to miss her," Stone said.

"Wretched excess," he replied.

"It's what Russians do with stolen money."

"Quite right."

They were silent for a moment. "What would you do with stolen money?" Stone asked, to pass the time.

"Hide it somewhere and buy better scotch and wines, then drink the evidence," Perce replied. "I see a blonde and a redhead with shopping bags."

"Those are ours," Stone said, making to rise.

"Stay where you are," Perce commanded. "Let's see where they go next. Are you expecting either of them to drop or pick up something?"

"Nothing they can't get in a store."

"And that's a lot," Dino said.

"I apologize for my friend," Stone said. "He's very rich, but he hasn't gotten used to it yet."

"I understand that. My wife's family had money, and I've still got most of it. I did spring for a nice Concordia."

"I've got one of those, in Maine," Stone said.

"I heard somebody's big yacht turned it into toothpicks in a fog," Perce said.

"That happened, but the offenders replaced it with an even nicer one."

"Lucky you."

"Where did they go?" Dino asked.

"Into the art gallery on your right," Perce said.

"Wake up, Dino," Stone chimed in.

"What for? There are two other sets of eyes on the job."

The three of them sat for another hour, watching the women enter and depart every other shop in sight, then turn toward them, festooned with shopping bags.

"See you at six-thirty," Perce said, then got up and disappeared into the afternoon crowd.

Stone and Dino watched them pass, ignoring their men, then walk out onto the dock where *Breeze* lay.

The women were already sipping something tropical-looking when Stone and Dino returned to the yacht. The two men accepted their usuals from a stewardess. "We'll be two more for dinner," Stone said to her. "The pilots will dine with you."

They finished their drinks then went to change. Stone wore his reefer suit, with a little diamond and sapphire replica of the Royal Yacht Squadron burgee stuck in his black necktie. Everybody else wore Sunday best.

They had hardly gotten settled when the stewardess announced, "Mr. Percy Willard and Ms. Christina Cabot." They
shook hands, sat down, and were brought drinks. "She's a cousin of
our acquaintance," Perce confided to Stone.

Christina Cabot was a striking woman of, perhaps, fifty, with
beautiful gray hair setting off her tan. Her breasts swelled under a
strapless white dress.

Stone noticed that Perce had an earpiece in his left ear, and he
suspected it was not a hearing aid.

"What do you hear from *Tsarina*?" Stone asked him.

Perce nodded toward a small group of people walking down
the dock to where a large tender awaited them and their luggage.
The McIntoshes and Betty Baker led the way.

"Vanessa?" Stone said quietly, then nodded toward the group,
as the tender took them away.

"Well," Vanessa said. "It's a relief to know where they are."

56

They dined on Caesar salad and two sliced porterhouse steaks, with haricots verts and roasted fingerling potatoes, and dessert was apple pie à la mode.

The ladies went to the powder room and Dino took a turn around the deck. Perce Willard came and sat down next to Stone, and they were served coffee and brandy. "I can't figure out who the hell you are," he said. "You're sitting here on this gorgeous yacht, with a stickpin in your tie that says you're a member of the Squadron, and a bakery heiress on your arm. I know you have a fancy title at the Agency, but you don't really work there. And nobody I know has any idea what you do. What the hell do you do, Stone?"

"What do *you* do for the Agency, Perce?" Stone parried.

"Whatever Lance Cabot asks me to do," Perce answered.

"Same here," Stone replied. "And she's not an heiress, she's a working woman who got poisoned recently by somebody on that yacht outside the harbor."

"I know what I get out of this," Perce said. "I'm seventy, and I get to stay on salary instead of taking my pension, and Lance gives me the title of station chief, which bumps up my civil service grade a notch or two, and I get to fuck his beautiful cousin two or three times a week. What are you getting out of it?"

"Pretty much what you get, except for the part about the beautiful cousin," Stone said. "And, of course, like you, I get the opportunity to serve my country now and then."

"Just what service are we providing our country right now? Are we supposed to do something to that giant yacht with the Russian name? I mean, I've got an Agency-owned Colt 1911 in my sock drawer, but they haven't issued me a limpet mine, yet. And even if they did, one of those people aboard is the acting secretary of state, so we can't blow *him* up." He thought for a moment. "Can we?"

"Not unless Lance tells us to," Stone replied. "But let me bring you up to date: the acting secretary and his wife, who has an important job at the Pentagon, may very well be active Russian spies, and Betty Baker, Vanessa's mother, may very well be who's running them."

Perce stared at him. "A Russian mole is running State?"

"Very possibly."

"So what are these people doing here—planning a Russian invasion of Martha's Vineyard?"

Stone laughed. "Probably not, Perce. Suffice to say, they're up to no good, and Lance wants to know just what that is."

"Oh, is that all? It sounds like we're going to have to make something up, just to keep Lance happy."

"I hope it doesn't come to that," Stone said. "I think all we can do is to report their actions, if any, to Lance, and let him figure it out."

"Well, my guess is that, right now, they're doing pretty much what we're doing. Maybe we should anchor out there next to them, then we can watch each other do it."

"I believe that you and I are not the only ones who are observing them," Stone said. "Let's wait and see what our invisible colleagues turn up. Maybe it will be something we can act on."

"Well," Perce said. "'Let's wait and see' has always been my personal credo. What's yours?"

"I think maybe I'll adopt yours, Perce," Stone replied. "It has the virtue of being optimistic—and not requiring any immediate action."

Dino came back from his stroll, the women reappeared from the powder room, and they all sat down to wait and see.

Vanessa came and sat next to Stone, snuggling up. "I think you're not very happy with me," she said.

"*Au contraire,*" Stone replied, searching for a place to rest his hand and finding an attractive thigh. "Just being with you makes me happy. You are, however, withholding something from me that, if I knew what it was, might make it easier to protect you from whatever you're frightened of."

"I understand," she replied, squeezing his hand and moving it farther up her thigh. "Let me explain as well as I can, while still keeping a promise."

"Please do."

"Not long after I was moved home from the hospital, before I could speak, I found I could listen and understand what others were saying, even though I appeared unconscious to them. During that time, Mother had a visitor, Yevgeny Chekhov. He came into my room, looked at me, and pinched me—hard. I did not respond, because I couldn't even wince. I then heard Mother come in and Chekhov said, 'Perhaps I should send someone around to complete this task.'

"Mother said, 'Not necessary. Her doctors have told me she can neither hear nor see, nor understand anything said to her.' There was a little tremor in her voice that he didn't catch, but I know well. It is always there when she is lying.

"There was a very long silence, then he said, 'As you wish, but if that turns out not to be the case, you will have to personally deal with the consequences.'"

"Do you think, then, that Betty is somehow in cahoots with Chekhov?" Stone asked.

"I'm sorry," Vanessa said. "Did I not mention that this conversation was conducted in Russian?"

"Betty speaks Russian?"

"Fluently. She studied the language and literature at Harvard, and she encouraged Mac McIntosh to study there, too."

"And you speak Russian?"

"Schoolgirl Russian. But I understand it quite well."

"Does Chekhov know that?"

"No. They often spoke Russian when together, and he took no notice of me when they did."

"Could you hear what they said to each other on that visit?"

"I could and did."

"Can you tell me the contents of that conversation?"

"No, I can't. It must have occurred to Mother that I heard them, because the next day, when I was beginning to speak a little, she extracted a promise from me not to tell anyone what she and Chekhov said to each other—on pain of death, hers and mine."

"Did what they said to each other constitute a threat to this country?"

"That's a sneaky question," she said.

"I'm a sneaky guy," he replied.

"No, not really."

"Not a good answer."

"Then no, they did not threaten the country. It was more benign than that."

"I should tell you that your government is treating their presence on this island as a very serious threat."

"I have no knowledge that it is their intention to threaten my country."

"And yet . . ."

"I'm afraid we'll have to leave it at that," she said.

57

As they began to move toward their cabins at bedtime, Stone stood to say good night to Dino and Viv. Viv took him aside and whispered, "I haven't had a chance to tell you, but when we were ashore shopping, I saw Betty Baker through a side window, and she and Vanessa saw each other."

"How do you know they did?"

"Because Betty winked at her, and Vanessa winked back. Good night, Stone."

Vanessa walked across the room from her chair. "I'm going to turn in," she said to Stone. "Don't be long."

Perce and Christina were still there, and Perce asked for the head. Stone directed him, then sat on the sofa, a cushion away from Christina.

"Would you like another cognac?" he asked.

"I think I'd better not," she replied. "I might become too bold."

"You may be as bold as you like," Stone said, pouring her another.

"I find you attractive," she said, placing a hand on his.

"What a nice coincidence," he said. "I find you attractive, too. Do you ever come to New York?"

"I live in New York," she said, "on Park Avenue, in the sixties."

"How convenient. I'm in Turtle Bay." He gave her his card. "Will you let me know when you're back?"

"Of course," she said, tucking the card into her bra, and offering her own card from the other side of the bra.

There was the distant noise of a vacuum toilet flushing; she withdrew her hand, and Stone put her card into his jacket's ticket pocket.

Perce came out and walked over. "Shall we?" he asked, extending his hand to help her from the sofa.

Stone stood up with her. "Good night, Perce. Good night, Christina," he said.

She rewarded him with a little smile. "Good night, Stone," she said, then followed Perce to the boarding stairs.

Stone stood at the top, watching them descend to the dock and, in so doing, caught an inviting glimpse of breasts, causing a stir in his loins.

He went below and found Vanessa naked in bed. He undressed and joined her.

She took him in her hand. "My, you've anticipated me," she said.

"You could say that," he replied, then moved into her.

The following morning they joined the Bacchettis at breakfast. They served themselves from the buffet, then sat down.

"What does the day hold?" Viv asked.

"What would you like to do? More shopping?"

"We'd like to take a closer look at that giant yacht outside the harbor," Dino said, clearly trying to deflect her interest.

"Why not?" Viv asked.

"Vanessa, would you like to see the giant yacht?"

"I'm a little tired this morning," she replied. "I think I'll have a nap after breakfast, then join you for lunch."

After breakfast Stone asked Captain Brett to put a tender from the upper deck into the water.

"Would you like a driver?" Brett asked.

"No, I'll do it myself."

A beautifully varnished runabout was winched down from the upper deck, and they boarded. Stone started the engine, and they moved away from the marina. They dodged the Chappaquiddick ferry, then followed the channel out of the inner harbor. Once outside, Stone applied more throttle, then headed toward *Tsarina* in the distance at a moderate speed. As they moved along, they were overtaken by a larger runabout with a half dozen people aboard. Stone accelerated and followed. "Dino," he said, "please take out your phone and get me a couple of pictures of the boat ahead. I'll pass them closely. I especially want faces."

"Sure," Dino said, producing his iPhone.

Stone increased their speed, and Dino did his work, then Stone peeled away from the other boat and headed for open water. Dino got a couple of shots of the big yacht as the people from the other tender climbed the boarding stairs.

Dino came and sat by Stone. "What do you want me to do with these pictures?" he asked.

"Send them to Lance's cell number," Stone replied, "and to mine."

They drove along the shore for a few minutes, then turned back toward the harbor. They were climbing aboard *Breeze* when Stone's phone rang. He answered it and scrambled, then found a chair.

"Good morning, Lance."

"Good morning, Stone. I trust you're enjoying yourself."

"We are, and we met a cousin of yours last evening."

"Ah, Christina. She's something, isn't she?"

"Quite something. Have you looked at Dino's photography?"

"The pictures are being fondled by some of our photographic experts. I'll have them shortly. That's some yacht, isn't it?"

"It is. Our captain tells us it's three hundred forty feet."

"Three hundred forty-five feet," Lance said. "We've researched her. She was launched last year at Abeking & Rasmussen, in Germany, a very fine yard. I'll e-mail you her layout, if you have a printer onboard."

"I do," Stone said.

"It might come in useful. Ah, here are the enlargements of Dino's photographs." Stone could hear a shuffling of papers and other voices in the room. "I don't have any names for you yet, but of the five people in the group, at least one of the men is GRU, and so is one of the women." The GRU was Russian military intelligence. "There was some luggage, so they must have just gotten off the ferry or an airplane."

"I wonder why they're here," Stone said.

"I may have something on that later in the day," Lance replied. "Oh, I've sent you a gift package, a tool kit, you might say. Be careful where you open it and don't leave the contents lying about." He hung up.

"Does Lance find my photography interesting?" Dino asked.

"He finds it fascinating," Stone said. "He's already spotted two GRU people among the visitors. He says he'll get back to us with more later in the day."

"I'll be interested to hear what he learns," Dino said.

Stone's phone rang; an e-mail from Lance. "Excuse me, I want to print some pages." He went to the little study on the yacht, where there lived a computer, and printed out several pages. Then he returned to Dino and Viv. Vanessa was just coming up from below, freshly dressed in a summery frock. He gave her a kiss. "Welcome back to the world," he said.

He and Dino spread the pages on a table. "Where did you get these shots of the interior and the drawings?" Dino asked.

"Lance produced them all," Stone said, poring over the pages. "It's as spectacular down below as it is on the upper decks," he said.

"Where'd Lance get these?"

"Probably hacked the builders' computer," Stone said.

They were interrupted by a call to lunch.

58

Lunch was Stone's favorite, a huge lobster salad that fed the whole table, washed down with a marvelous white burgundy. They had just moved to the fantail for coffee when Perce turned up tugging a lightweight luggage cart, holding a single box, taped shut.

"A delivery for you," Perce said to Stone, "by way of me."

"Sit down, Perce, and have some coffee and coconut cake," Stone said. "I'll open it later."

Perce abandoned the cart in favor of dessert. "Christina told me to tell you she greatly enjoyed last evening," he said between bites. "This is wonderful cake," he said. "Was it baked by Vanessa?"

"No, it was baked by the Peninsula Grill, in Charleston, and sent to me by a friend. You're right, it is wonderful."

Dino spoke for the others. "We're going to take a dingy and do some shell fishing for our supper. Would you like to come along, Stone?"

"Thanks, no, I've got to talk to Perce."

The other three changed into their swimsuits and left the yacht in the rubber dinghy.

"Does Dino know where he's going?" Perce asked.

"He does. He's been there before."

"Time to open your present from Lance," Perce said. "It's too heavy for me, at my age."

Stone lifted the box off the cart and set it on the coffee table. "Heavier than it looks," he said.

Perce handed him a Swiss Army knife.

Stone hacked through the wrapping and strapping and took off the lid. "Some tool kit," he said to Perce.

He spread a towel over the glass top and began removing tools. There were a pair of pistols with a dozen loaded magazines; two silencers; two handheld radios and a charger; a box of extra pistol ammo; a pair of short-handled bolt cutters; and two holsters with assorted screwdrivers and other small tools. "Did Lance mention what he wanted us to do with all this?" Stone asked, drily.

Perce laughed. "It looks like an instant boarding and destruction kit, with a little assassination on the side."

"Well, Perce," Stone said, "I'm not boarding anything more boisterous than that rubber dinghy Dino just sailed away, and I'm not destroying anything, either, or shooting anybody."

"And there's no limpet mine enclosed," Perce said.

"I think this is just Lance's idea of a little joke."

"I've never known Lance to joke about something like this. I think he expects these tools to be used."

"Then Lance will have to get his ass up to the Vineyard and use them himself."

"Done," a voice said, lifting Stone off his chair. He looked up to find Lance standing at the top of the boarding ladder. "Permission to come aboard?" He gave them a stiff, British salute.

"If you must," Stone replied. "Can I get you a drink?"

Lance disported himself on the sofa. "A little early for me. Perhaps after our little swim tonight."

"If you're taking a swim tonight," Stone said, "I'll be happy to stand on the fantail and wave you off."

"Only joking about the swim," Lance replied. "Anyway, I'm leery of swimming in water that isn't chlorinated, and I'm told that this is a particularly good year for great white sharks in Vineyard waters."

"I saw something on the news about that," Stone said, "and I am not encouraged."

Perce spoke up. "Did I mention that I'm too old for swimming?"

"No need, Perce," Lance said.

"Oh, good. I was about to submit my retirement papers."

"Don't worry, Perce," Lance said. "You'll continue to get your paychecks from us, and you're still on Christina's active list."

"You make me sound like a gigolo, Lance," Perce replied tartly. "Though it is flattering to think that a beautiful woman might pay for my services."

"Christina says that your presence keeps the flies away from the honey."

A shout came up from the dock. "Ahoy, *Breeze*," a male voice called out.

Lance got up and walked over to the rail. "This one's for me," he said, beckoning to somebody below.

Two young men, dressed in tight shorts and T-shirts that showed off their muscles, came up the steps and shook Lance's hand.

"Stone, meet Ben and Jerry," Lance said.

"Are they delivering ice cream?" Stone asked.

"No, they've come to collect their tools," Lance said.

Stone returned the tools to the toolbox and pushed it toward them. "All yours, fellas."

"You're not going to offer us a drink?" Ben asked.

"Not at this hour," Lance said. "And I believe you're late for your briefing."

Jerry picked up the toolbox by its handle, disdaining the luggage cart, and the two marched down the ladder and up the dock.

"You see," Lance said, "I did not expect derring-do from either of you."

"And that's the only reason you're not great white bait," Stone said.

Lance returned to his spot on the sofa. "Perhaps I'll have just a taste of that pitcher of Bloody Awfuls on the bar," he said.

Perce poured one for him and handed him the icy glass and a napkin. "There you go," he said.

"Lance," Stone said, "to what do we owe the pleasure of your company?"

"There's a meeting being held aboard *Tsarina* this evening, and thanks to Dino's holiday snaps, I know who's attending. Now I want to know what is said."

"How do you expect to learn that?" Stone asked.

"That will be the fruit of Ben and Jerry's work last night," Lance replied, "and I hope I may impinge on your hospitality until tomorrow morning, because this yacht is moored in the spot where the best possible reception can be obtained without attracting attention."

"Well," Stone said, "since swimming with sharks is not required of your host, we are happy to receive you."

Lance sipped his drink. "I suppose you want to know more, Stone."

"You are very perceptive, Lance. You could begin by telling me who the attendees of tonight's meeting are."

"All right," Lance said. "I don't see any harm in that."

"May I listen, too?" Perce asked.

"Of course, Perce," Lance said. "After all, if not for you, we would not be here."

"Come on, Lance," Stone said. "Cough it up."

"Certainly," Lance replied. "The attendees are all nine of the GRU's agents implanted on our country's Eastern Seaboard, three of them native-born Americans."

59

S tone was stunned. This had snuck up on him. He had been expecting something less. "Are you going to arrest them?" he asked Lance.

"That decision will be made at a level above my pay grade," Lance replied.

"Lance," Stone responded, "you are the director of the Central Intelligence Agency. There is no one above your pay grade."

"My betters reside in the halls of government—committee chairmen and the like."

Stone knew that "the like" included President Katharine Lee, and probably would have included Holly Barker, if she were still employed by the government, instead of campaigning in Iowa.

"Do the people aboard that yacht have any idea that you know what you know about them?" Stone asked.

"I hope to learn that tonight, after they've had a few drinks. If they do know, they'll be scooped up before dawn. If not, we may release them into the wild and allow them to go on doing their work, albeit through filters placed by us in their stream of knowledge."

Stone was surprised. "You mean you'd leave Mac McIntosh at State?"

"Mac and Laura McIntosh came to see me the other day," Lance said. "If the decision is made to replace Mac at State, then a candidate—already agreed upon by Kate and Holly, if she's elected—will fill the job and remain in it after the inauguration. Mac and Laura, on the other hand, will be provided with a cushy, sealed-off corner of the Agency where they can ply their trade with carefully sanitized intelligence that they can pass on to their superiors."

"And if Holly loses?"

"By that time the McIntoshes will already be working for us, thanks to your little improvisation over lunch with them at the Grill."

"What about Betty?" Stone asked.

"Betty will be allowed to go on doing what she has been doing, but under constant surveillance. Recruiting is one of her tasks. She recruited Peter Grant and the McIntoshes. We'll see that she has opportunities to choose among a group of carefully vetted people, who will pass information to her that she will, of course, pass on to the GRU."

"False information."

"Let's call it freshly laundered and ironed," Lance said.

"But then there's Vanessa," Stone pointed out.

"What about her?"

"What will you do with her?"

Lance gave a little shrug. "Nothing. She and Betty were never in cahoots, and are estranged. You will let her know that it's best for both her and her mother to remain so. After all, Vanessa has a business to run, and she will give the chop to her mother quite soon, probably asking you, as her attorney, to wield the axe."

"Fine by me," Stone said.

"Vanessa is never to know what happens here during the next twenty-four hours. Is that clear? The 'never' part, I mean."

"It's clear. And what part do I play in what happens tonight?"

"Your part is to take Vanessa to bed and exhaust her, so that she does not wake until the sun is high. You will be assisted in your task by this." Lance reached into the watch pocket of his trousers and produced a tiny, zipped plastic envelope containing two small pills. "One in her drink will dissolve quickly. And in about twenty minutes, she'll want to sleep."

"What's the other one for?" Stone asked.

"That's for if one doesn't quite do the trick—or, if it does, you can have it for yourself."

"What is it?"

"A small dose of a common prescription sleeping pill, nothing dramatic."

Stone tucked the envelope into his own watch pocket.

"I think you should take the pill in any case, Stone," Lance said. "It will suppress your curiosity about tonight's activities."

"You don't want me to know what happens?"

"It's more that you don't *need* to know," Lance said. "What you don't know can't hurt you."

"When is all this going to happen?"

"I'd like you and your party tucked up and asleep by midnight," Lance said.

"And where will you be?"

"On your upper deck, sheltered in your larger tender, listening and recording. Discourage anyone who makes a move to go up there. There'll be a man ashore with a sniper's rifle, to make sure I'm not disturbed."

"I'll see to it that no one disturbs you."

Lance handed him another little envelope with two more pills inside. "For Dino and Viv. Insist, if you have to."

"Will you join us for dinner?"

"If all goes smoothly, yes, but don't count on me."

Dinner was a big pot of paella, made with the group's catch of shellfish. Lance turned up just as they were finishing drinks.

"Nothing to drink for me," Lance said. "I'm too hungry to drink."

They moved to the dining table and took the lid off the pot, flooding the night with a delicious smell. Everybody had seconds.

After dinner, they moved to the fantail for coffee and dessert, and Lance took the opportunity to pull Stone aside. "Don't take your pill tonight. I'm going to need you. One of my lads got a bad oyster and is incapable."

"No swimming," Stone said.

"No swimming, but wear dark clothing, nothing white. Come up to the top deck as soon as Vanessa is sound asleep. You might give her both pills."

Then they sat down for coffee and freshly baked carrot cake.

"Mmmm," Lance said, tasting his. "Good for one's night vision." He winked at Stone.

60

tone exhausted Vanessa and saw her finish a small glass of Grand Marnier with a pill dissolved in it. Then, tired himself, he drifted off.

He was shaken and awakened before midnight. "Get dressed and come up top," Lance whispered.

Stone shook off sleep and got into the dark blue clothing he had laid out, then ran lightly to the top deck, where a crewman was ready to launch one of the tenders. Lance was already sitting in it; Stone joined him, and they were gently lowered into the water. The town was fairly darkened, and only the masthead lights of yachts at moorings lit the harbor.

"Put this on," Lance said, handing him a balaclava, a knit cap that revealed only his eyes. Lance passed him a pair of goggles. "Night vision," Lance said, and showed him the switch. "Don't use them until we're out of the harbor. You're driving." He pointed at the controls and switched on the key. "It's electric, very quiet. Once we're out of the harbor, go slowly and don't make a wake."

Stone took the controls and put a lever into the forward position. Lance was right; it was very quiet.

"How much range have we got?" Stone asked.

"It's fully charged, so about sixty miles at cruise speed, much more at our pace."

They passed the entrance to the harbor, and they pulled on the night-vision goggles and switched them on. "Don't look back at the harbor or the town," Lance said. "That would screw up your night vision."

The goggles were excellent. Stone could see everything he could see in daylight, but with a green tinge. He saw crab-trap buoys and navigational markers. And there sat *Tsarina,* wearing a single light at the top of the mast. On the upper decks small lamps burned, and Lance reached out and adjusted the goggles so that they would not ruin his night vision. Even candles, burning on the rear deck, showed bright.

Lance handed Stone an earpiece. "It's already on, and you can adjust the volume with the little wheel."

Stone pulled up his balaclava to expose his ear, stuck in the piece, and pulled the headgear back into place. Immediately, he could hear voices, as clearly as if the people were sitting in the boat with them.

Lance pulled the power lever back to the idle position, and the boat slowed, making even less noise. Stone turned his attention to the conversation. It was in Russian.

"Well, shit," he said to nobody in particular.

"Get up close to her hull, then work around to the stern," Lance said.

Stone did so, staying under the overhang of the rear deck, where the party was drinking. Lance found some sort of protrusion from the hull and got the painter around it. The tide was going out, so the runabout stayed downstream of her, still under the overhang.

Suddenly, Stone heard English. "I'm afraid my Russian is a bit rusty," the voice of Betty Baker said. "Do you mind if we speak English?"

"Not at all," the voice of Yevgeny Chekhov replied in English. "We all speak English here." They droned on with small talk, and Stone grew drowsy.

Stone did not know how much time had passed before Lance jabbed at his thigh with a hard object. He snapped to, and sat very still. A small outboard motor could be heard. It got farther away, then apparently, came around the bow of the big yacht and started aft, because it was getting louder. Clearly, someone was looking for someone else, like Stone and Lance. "How fast will this thing go?" he whispered to Lance.

"I'm letting go of this line. Drive all the way around the yacht slowly, keeping her on your right, until we get back here." Lance pulled the painter aboard, and Stone did as he was told. Halfway up the port side of the hull, they came to a boarding ladder with a small pontoon affixed to it. "Don't stop," Lance said. "We're not going aboard."

"You're damned right we're not," Stone said, speeding up slightly. They were around the bow and headed astern before they heard the outboard stop, apparently at the boarding ladder.

"Back to where we were," Lance said, and Stone complied. Shortly, they were tied up astern again.

The group at the stern was making noises about turning in, mostly in Russian, then Stone heard Betty's voice again.

"Yevgeny, may I speak to you for a moment?"

"Of course," Chekhov said.

"It's about Vanessa. I want you to know that you have nothing to fear from her."

"I'm glad to hear that, Betty."

"I've moved out of her apartment, back into my own place, and I'll be leaving her company when I get back."

"Yes?"

"The two of us are not on speaking terms at the moment. I want your personal assurance that nothing will happen to her."

"You're sure about this?"

"Absolutely. She and I have never discussed anything about our arrangement. The poison was a great mistake."

"That was Peter's doing. He didn't ask me."

"The only time you and I have discussed our relationship around her was when she was unconscious. I made sure of that."

"I will take your word for that, Betty, on one condition: If she ever mentions our relationship, you must let me know immediately. Will you promise to do that?"

"I do promise, Yevgeny."

"Then let's get to bed," he said. "You'll be awakened early in the morning. The plane will be ready for us at ten o'clock."

They went below. Stone could still hear them when they said good night.

"Time to go," Lance said, freeing the painter.

Stone switched on the engine, put it in forward, and pointed it more or less south, in the direction of the harbor. They were, perhaps, a hundred yards from the yacht when Stone suddenly went blind.

"Jesus!" Lance said, ripping off his goggles and Stone's, too. They heard an outboard start, a bigger one than before.

"I can't see a thing," Stone said.

"Spotlight," Lance said. "You were pointed at the harbor before, so keep that heading. Just go faster. Your vision will gradually come back."

Stone groped for the lever and shoved it halfway forward, the boat leaping. "How fast can we go?"

"Forty knots, but not for very long," Lance said. "Can you see anything yet?"

Stone blinked his eyes rapidly. "Not yet."

"Can you see our compass?" Lance asked.

"I think so."

Lance reached down and moved the throttle all the way forward, while Stone held on to the wheel for dear life.

"Just keep the heading we were on," Lance said.

"Right up until we come to a sudden stop," Stone replied, "like, against a big rock."

He heard something whistle past them in the air. "Bullet," he said.

"Silenced weapon," Lance replied.

The next one went through their windshield. Stone could see the compass now; he was off course but corrected.

61

The windshield took another round, making it harder to see
through, but now Stone could make out the masthead lights
in the harbor and the tall light at the marina, a couple miles
away.

Lance looked back. "No further pursuit, but we're blown. Time
for Plan Zero." He picked up his radio and spoke into it. "Plan
Zero. Plan Zero. Plan Zero. Execute. There will be small arms
fire."

Stone steered toward *Breeze* now. He could see her clearly by
the marina lights. "What's Plan Zero?" he asked. A helicopter flew
down the harbor at low altitude; lights were coming on aboard
yachts.

"Plan Zero is to board *Tsarina* and capture all persons. No
shooting unless absolutely necessary."

"How far into the future does Plan Zero take us?"

"Until dawn," Lance said. "Everyone who's still alive will
be transported to a secure facility; any wounded or dead will be
attended to. Once secured, interrogation of those on board will

commence. That will be helped along by the fact that we've recorded everything anyone on board has said for the past two days."

Stone pulled up to the outboard side of *Breeze*, caught the hoisting cables, and hooked them up. "What can I tell Vanessa about her mother's fate?"

"You can tell her that Betty has been detained for questioning. She'll be given an opportunity to speak to an attorney. Then, if she tells all and agrees to testify, she won't do more than a year of prison time, and that at the nearest thing we have to a country club prison."

"And if she doesn't?"

"She's our best shot, since she's an American and has a life to go back to, unlike the others. If she doesn't accept the plea deal, then she, along with all the others, will be transported to a *very* secure location, the name of which you would recognize but I can't speak it."

"Sounds like Guantánamo," Stone muttered.

"I didn't say that, and you didn't hear it," Lance said.

The runabout was hoisted onto the top deck by a winch and set gently into a cradle. Stone and Lance gathered their equipment and dropped it into a canvas bag that Lance produced. He kept his radio.

An edge of the sun seemed to rise from Chappaquiddick, to the east. They went down to the main deck, looking for breakfast. A crew member took their order.

"Lance," Stone said, "why are you here? I mean, raiding foreign yachts and capturing their passengers is not part of your job description, is it?"

"My job description is whatever I want it to be, and once in a while, I like to get out into the weeds with operational people. It's more fun than sitting behind a desk."

Lance's radio crackled. "Scramble," he said.

"Scrambled," came the reply.

"What is your status?" Lance asked.

"Plan Zero executed and complete. We're returning to mother ship."

"Casualties?"

"One wounded in our party, non-life-threatening. Two wounded, one female fatality among the detainees."

"Which female?" Lance asked.

"Number one," he replied. "It couldn't be helped. She was given every opportunity, but she shot our guy."

"Secure," Lance said. "Over and out." He dropped the radio into the canvas bag with the other gear.

"Who is female one?" Stone asked.

"I could lie to you but I'd rather not. It's Betty Baker."

Stone sighed, making a moaning noise. "Oh, God," he said.

The two of them had finished breakfast when Dino and Viv appeared on deck, hungry.

"You two been up all night?" Dino asked.

"Most of it," Stone said.

"Is Vanessa up?" Lance asked.

"I could hear her moving about when we came up," Viv replied.

"Stone," Lance said. "You'd better go and speak to her."

Stone turned and looked at him askance.

"She's yours," Lance said, "and your work to do. Don't lie to her, but tell her as little as possible."

Stone felt as if he had been struck in the chest with a heavy object, but he got unsteadily to his feet and headed for the stairs, feeling sick.

END

Mount Desert Island, Maine

July 12, 2019

AUTHOR'S NOTE

I am happy to hear from readers, but you should know that if you write to me in care of my publisher, three to six months will pass before I receive your letter, and when it finally arrives it will be one among many, and I will not be able to reply.

However, if you have access to the Internet, you may visit my website at www.stuartwoods.com, where there is a button for sending me e-mail. So far, I have been able to reply to all my e-mail, and I will continue to try to do so.

If you send me an e-mail and do not receive a reply, it is probably because you are among an alarming number of people who have entered their e-mail address incorrectly in their mail software. I have many of my replies returned as undeliverable.

Remember: e-mail, reply; snail mail, no reply.

When you e-mail, please do not send attachments, as I never open these. They can take twenty minutes to download, and they often contain viruses.

Please do not place me on your mailing lists for funny stories, prayers, political causes, charitable fund-raising, petitions, or sentimental claptrap. I get enough of that from people I already know.

Generally speaking, when I get e-mail addressed to a large number of people, I immediately delete it without reading it.

Please do not send me your ideas for a book, as I have a policy of writing only what I myself invent. If you send me story ideas, I will immediately delete them without reading them. If you have a good idea for a book, write it yourself, but I will not be able to advise you on how to get it published. Buy a copy of *Writer's Market* at any bookstore; that will tell you how.

Anyone with a request concerning events or appearances may e-mail it to me or send it to: Publicity Department, Penguin Publishing Group, 1745 Broadway, New York, NY 10019.

Those ambitious folk who wish to buy film, dramatic, or television rights to my books should contact Matthew Snyder, Creative Artists Agency, 9830 Wilshire Boulevard, Beverly Hills, CA 98212-1825.

Those who wish to make offers for rights of a literary nature should contact Anne Sibbald, Janklow & Nesbit, 285 Madison Avenue, New York, NY 10022. (Note: This is not an invitation for you to send her your manuscript or to solicit her to be your agent.)

If you want to know if I will be signing books in your city, please visit my website, www.stuartwoods.com, where the tour schedule will be published a month or so in advance. If you wish me to do a book signing in your locality, ask your favorite bookseller to contact his Penguin representative or the Penguin publicity department with the request.

If you find typographical or editorial errors in my book and feel an irresistible urge to tell someone, please write to Sara Minnich at Penguin's address above. Do not e-mail your discoveries to me, as I will already have learned about them from others.

A list of my published works appears in the front of this book and on my website. All the novels are still in print in paperback and can be found at or ordered from any bookstore. If you wish to obtain hardcover copies of earlier novels or of the two nonfiction books, a good used-book store or one of the online bookstores can help you find them. Otherwise, you will have to go to a great many garage sales.